WITCHIN' IMPOSSIBLE

SEMI-COZY PARANORMAL FUN

WITCHIN' IMPOSSIBLE MYSTERIES
BOOK 1

RENEE GEORGE

BARKSIDE OF THE MOON PRESS

Witchin' Impossible: Witchin' Impossible Cozy Mysteries Book 1

Copyright © 2018 by Renee George

Print ISBN-13: 978-1-947177-24-6

Publisher: Barkside of the Moon Press

For my sister Robbin.
You are always there for me.
You are the best, my darling,
even when I'm bratty.
And for the other awesome Robyn in my life,
You are a miracle in friendship.
Thank you for all you do and are.

ACKNOWLEDGMENTS

A special THANK YOU to the fabulous Robyn Peterman, an awesomely funny writer, and my favorite cookie, for allowing me the privilege to write in her world. And thank you for giving me back the rights to rework the story and place it in my own world when the KW hit the skids. I love you, Cookie!

Also, I must thank the usual suspects, my BFF sister and most fabulous beta reader Robbin, my BFF, and critique partner Michele Bardsley, and my BFF and the person who talks me off the ledge, Dakota Cassidy. You guys are like the chocolate to my almonds, the butter to my toast, and the sweetener to my tea. I love you like I love my left leg.

To my Rebels, you all RAWK! You keep me going every day with your support. I love you to the moon and back.

To my fans, I would not be anything without you. Seriously. If you keep reading, I'll keep writing! Thank you. Thank you. Thank you. If I were reviewing you all, you would get five-gazillion stars and a million-gazillion smooches.

Oh! And lest I forget, thank you strong, black coffee. Without you, I couldn't get out of bed in the morning, let alone write a single word.

Sometimes you can't go home, and that would've been just fine by me.

I'm Hazel Kinsey, a special agent for the FBI, and I'm also a witch. Seventeen years earlier, I packed up my belongings and my squirrel familiar Tizzy, and I left my paranormal hometown of Paradise Falls for good. Or so I thought.

When my best friend from high school, Lily Mason, calls and asks me to investigate her brother's murder, I can't say no. She was there for me during the worst time of my life, and it's my turn to return the favor, no matter the personal cost.

Going home is harder than I imagined. My grumpy, hot high school crush, a bear shifter named Ford Baylor, has become a grumpy, hot police officer who's not happy to see me.

Unfortunately, I can't stop thinking about him. All these years away, I imagined him married to his bear shifter sweetheart and living the white-picket-fence dream. But Ford is single, and he looks ready to strangle me.

Apparently, I'm his mate. Who knew?

On top of that, there's a sinister force at work in Paradise Falls, and I have to solve the mysterious murders happening around town if I want to prevent my best friend from becoming the next victim.

CHAPTER 1

"TIZZY!" I shouted.

A large red squirrel leap-frogged the couch and the loveseat, then slid across the dining room table. She grabbed a nut from a bowl in the center as she passed. Swiftly, she flew off the edge of the table and through the air the last couple of feet before coming to an abrupt halt in front of my coffee cup.

"You called?" She cracked the walnut on the counter and picked away at the shell with a pretty, pink-painted nail. Through all this, she barely glanced at me.

"Where did you put my Glock?" I tapped my own pretty, pink-painted nail on the hard counter. "And quit using all my polish."

She held out her tiny paw and examined her manicure. "I can't help it if I make this shade look good." Finally, she cast her large, dark brown eyes on me and batted her unnaturally thick lashes. "You're a witch, Hazel. You don't need a gun."

"I'm an FBI agent, Tizzy," I told her. "It's expected."

The squirrel turned around and swished her tail at me. "I worry about you, is all." When she turned back around, the nut she'd held was gone, and my pistol was magically on the counter in front of her. "Ta-dah!" She stretched out her arms, palms up, and wiggled her fingers.

I tried to keep my gaze disappointed, but when your flying squirrel familiar strikes a pose and gives you jazz hands, it's hard not to freaking smile. I grabbed the gun and holstered it on my belt. "Just leave the standard-issue FBI weapon alone. I'd hate to have to throw you in jail."

Tizzy clasped her hands together and held them over her heart. "Oh, Hazel," she said with great tragedy. "I am not made for a cage!"

I shook my head at her. "Calm down."

My phone rang as I contemplated putting my familiar on a mood stabilizer.

I pressed it to my ear. "Special Agent Kinsey."

"Haze?"

The quiet feminine voice startled me. "Lily?"

"It's me," she answered.

Lily Mason had been my best friend all through elementary and high school. We hadn't kept in touch. It had less to do with a falling out and more to do with the fact that when I left Paradise Falls (more like Paradise Fails), I never looked back. The memories were too painful. Even now, I felt trepidation like a cold trickle of sweat down my back.

"What's happened?" I asked.

I heard a choke of grief on her end. "Danny's dead."

Danny was Lily's younger brother. He had to be in his early twenties now. Her parents had died our senior year, and without any other family, she and Danny had been left to fend for themselves. Guilt tugged at me when I thought about what it must have been like for Lily. We'd both dreamed of escaping Paradise Falls, but Danny had been seven years old at the time. I'd already received my acceptance to Iowa University, so the minute I had my diploma in hand, I hightailed it out of town. I didn't even participate in the graduation ceremony. Lily, who had planned to go to the university with me, stayed behind to raise the kid.

I took a beat as the news sank in before asking, "How did he die?"

Lily and her brother were werecougars. Shifters. Their kind is immune to regular disease, so I braced myself for an unpleasant answer.

When she said, "Murdered. Someone or something killed him," I nearly swallowed my tongue.

"You're joking." Her silence was enough to make me feel like a total ass. "What do you need me to do?"

"The witches don't believe magic was involved, so they won't investigate."

"What about the shifters?"

"Danny has been in and out of trouble the last couple of years. Drugs. Fights. They think he's responsible for his own death. They won't act."

"Harvest in a hailstorm," I swore. "How long ago did it happen?"

"It's been four months now."

"Oh, honey. You should have called me."

"I'm calling now."

But not in time for me to go home for a funeral. For Goddess' sake. I really had been a rotten friend. "Do you suspect anyone?"

"I've checked with all his so-called friends and acquaintances. According to them, Danny hadn't pissed anyone off enough to take his life."

"How did he die?"

"The medical examiner said that every bone in his body had been broken."

I shook my head. "That wouldn't kill a shifter."

"No," she agreed. "But when his killer broke his ribs, one of them stabbed into his heart. In the end, that's why he died." Her voice trembled. "It was the very last bone. The examiner suspects it was meant to be a killing blow."

"I'm so sorry, Lily." The tragic circumstances of his death sounded more awful than my condolences could convey. I had to make this right for Lily. No way would I let her down again. "I'll check into Danny's death. The witches might not talk to you, but they'll talk to me."

"Haze," she said.

"Yeah?" I asked, already looking up my boss' phone number.

Lily was silent for a couple of seconds.

"Is there anything else I need to know?"

"Not about Danny," she answered quietly. "I'm… I'm glad you're coming. Anything you can do would be great."

A wave of guilt hit me again when I heard the relief in her voice. Lily had really been there for me during a rough time in my life. She'd encouraged me to get the hell out of town and get a fresh start. This phone conversation was a reminder that I hadn't just left my problems behind, I'd also left the one person I could always count on. "I'll call you back when I have news."

"Thanks, Haze."

"I can't promise anything, Lily. Just…well, hope for the best, prepare for the worst. I'll let you know as soon as I can get on my way there."

She hung up, but it took me a second to put the phone down. Little Danny Mason was dead, and my best friend was alone in her pursuit of justice.

I contacted my direct supervisor at the Kansas City office of the Federal Bureau of Investigation. I had to put in for emergency leave before making the call I'd dreaded the most. I punched in the number quickly, as if I were ripping off a bandage.

It went straight to voicemail, and my blood ran cold when I heard, "You've reached Grand Inquisitor Clementine Battles. Please leave your name and a number after the beep, and I will get back to you as soon as I can."

"Belch fire and save matches," I grumbled. I never mixed my business and witch life, but if I wanted to investigate a supernatural crime that possibly involved witches, I had to get permission from the old Battle-axe. I'd been so out of touch with the magical part of my life that I worried she would immediately turn me down.

I cringed as the phone beeped. "Uhm, this is Hazel. You probably don't want to hear from me, but could you call me at— Ah!" I jumped back, my hand automatically going for my holstered weapon.

Right in the middle of my living room, a silver-haired woman appeared wearing a figure-hugging navy-blue dress suit. Her silver hair was pulled back into a severe bun as she crossed her arms over her chest and stared at me sternly. "You called," she said, reminding me of Tizzy for a moment.

I pressed my fingertips to my chest. "You scared the crap out of me."

The last time I'd seen the Grand Inquisitor, she'd been directing a couple of her witch goons to transport my dad to prison. I'm pretty sure she'd worn the same outfit.

"I thought I smelled something foul," Tizzy said, waving her tiny fingers in front of her face.

"Tiz." I shook my head.

She rolled her eyes. The fact that my familiar wasn't more scared spoke volumes as to just how out of the witch loop I'd kept her.

Clementine Battles, who looked to be in her mid-thirties but was actually over two hundred years old, raised an appraising brow at the squirrel. "Tell me what you want, Hazel."

"Really. You could have just called me back," I told her. "That would have been totally cool."

"You have spent your whole adult life avoiding our world." She pulled out a tiny spiral memo book and flipped it open like a cop at a crime scene. "Here," she said, pointing at a tiny line of writing. "The last time you used magic for any real purpose, other than the negligible location spell every now and then, was in the spring of your eighteenth year, right before you left Paradise Falls. Do you even know how to spellcast anymore?"

"Yes," I said unconvincingly. Cripes, she was like the freaking Goddess with the whole "all-knowing" shtick.

She smiled, and I'd never seen anything scarier in my life. "I not only know everything, Hazel, but unlike the Goddess, I pay attention to everything as well."

Goose bumps rose on my arms as I felt the enormity of the Grand Inquisitor's power. Tizzy scampered under the couch, and for a second, I wondered if there was enough room for me.

The powerful witch snapped her fingers. "Now, tell me why, after nearly two decades, you are calling me for help."

"Because," I told her. "I *need* your help." I avoided making a "duh" gesture and continued. "I got a phone call from my friend Lily Mason, a shifter in Paradise Falls. Her brother's been killed, and she needs my help. Which means I need your permission to investigate Daniel Mason's death. It's the only way the witches in town will cooperate or at least not interfere." If it wasn't for Lily, I would've never called, but I kept that information to myself.

The Grand Inquisitor tapped her chin. "Granted."

My inner witch squeeed, but my outer agent kept a calm expression in place.

"However…"

My heart sank as my inner witch said, *well, crap*. "Okay," I said. "Let me have it."

"I would like you to be more involved in our community. I'm not asking you to leave the FBI, Hazel, but you can no longer act as if you live on Lone Witch Island. And…" She narrowed her gaze. "You will owe me a favor. A marker I can call in anytime I wish."

I thought about Lily—how desperate and bereaved she'd sounded on the phone. I didn't want to let her down, but turning myself into Clementine Battle's bitch was a hefty price to pay.

"Forget it." She waved me off with a quick flick of the wrist. "Permission denied."

"Wait!" I gripped the edge of my counter. "I'll do it."

She raised both brows. "You'll do what?"

"I'll be more involved with the witch community, and I'll owe you a favor."

"Two favors now."

My aggravation made my fingers spark. Channeling electricity was one of the first kinds of magic I'd mastered, and occasionally, when my frustration level rose, it manifested like static electricity. "Yes," I finally said. "Two favors."

"Also, I want you to address me properly."

I sighed. I knew what she wanted, but saying the words were difficult. Finally, I ground out, "Yes, Grandmother."

Did I forget to mention that the "Battle-axe" is my grandmother? But when she put my father—her only son—in jail, it sort of drove a wedge between us. Ugh. I hated that I needed her help.

"Correct answer, Granddaughter." She smiled, obviously pleased with herself, and produced a card. She handed it to me. "So mote it be."

I automatically recited back, "So mote it be," as I took the card. The small white rectangle had one word on it: Pass.

"What's this?"

"It's your *Get Out Of Jail Free* card. The witches of Paradise Falls will know it's from me."

"Thank—" Before I could finish, she poofed out. "Wow."

"No kidding," Tizzy said, still under the couch. "That is one terrifying witch!"

"Yes, she is," I agreed. "And you had to go and poke her. What was all that crap about a terrible smell? Do you have a death wish?"

She peeked her head out from under the couch and looked up at me. "You want me on my best behavior, then warn me the next time you invite her over."

"I didn't invite her." I tucked the white card into my wallet. "It doesn't matter. I'm alive. You're alive. Neither of us is in jail. And we have a murder to solve." In the last place on earth, I ever wanted to see again. "Come on," I told Tiz. "We've got packing to do."

She scurried up the couch until she was on top of the backrest and squealed her excitement.

"Seriously?" She fist-pumped the air. "Road trip!"

CHAPTER 2

"I DON'T KNOW why we don't just teleport," Tizzy complained for the umpteen-millionth time. "You're a witch going on witch business. Why did we have to drive?"

"It's only a five-hour drive, Tiz." I didn't want to admit that it had been so long since I'd teleported that I was afraid I'd land us in the middle of the Pacific Ocean. Besides, I didn't mind driving. "Quit being so dramatic," I added.

An almond shell whacked the side of my head.

"Stop that." I snatched the bag of nuts from Tizzy's lap.

Her already high voice went up an octave. "Giveemtomerightnow!"

"You be nice, and I'll be nice."

Her tiny lower lip trembled, and her large brown eyes widened.

"Oh fine." I gave her back the nuts. "You know. You're my familiar. You're supposed to serve me. Not the other way around."

Tizzy cracked another nut. "You start acting like a witch, and I'll start acting like a witch's familiar."

She sorta had a point. "I'm sorry, Tisiphone," I said, using her given name. "You deserved better than me."

She shrugged her furry shoulders. "It'll be nice to get back to Paradise Falls. There is a certain chipmunk shifter who I'm anxious to rekindle a flame with."

"Please tell me you're not talking about Jackie Stringer?" She was the only chipmunk shifter I knew in school.

Tiz's silence seemed to confirm my suspicion.

"Seriously?" Jackie had been one of those bubbly brainiacs. A combination of cutes and smarts that sometimes turned a girl mean. "She asked me if I was 'Hazed and confused' after I failed a history exam my sophomore year."

Tizzy smiled, her two front teeth shining bright and her eyes flashing with satisfaction. "What can I say?" Her expression was coy. "She kissed a squirrel, and she liked it."

"Oh, my Goddess. How did I not know this was happening right under my own nose?"

"You were a teenager, Haze. You couldn't see

anything that didn't involve you and all that angsty drama." She put the back of her hand to her forehead and struck a despondent pose. "Oh, Tiz, I love him so much, but he doesn't know I exist." She hit another pose. "Tizzy, I got an A-minus on my chemistry test. I want to die. Tiz, Mom won't let me go to a party with Lily. She is trying to kill my social life. Blah, blah, blah."

"I get it," I said, dismissing her antics. "So, Jackie Freaking Stringer."

"Haters gonna hate."

Her enthusiasm was like a wake-up call. In the years since I'd left Paradise Falls, I'd never really thought about what it had meant for Tizzy. She was always waiting for me at home. She'd kept herself hidden when I'd gone to the police academy and later when I'd had to stay at Quantico. Never in all that time did she complain about being lonely. But I could see real excitement on her face as we neared my old hometown. It was a joy I hadn't seen in her for so long that I didn't even know it was missing.

A sign ahead touted: Paradise Falls – 2 Miles. "We're almost there."

I got into the right-hand lane for the exit as Tizzy tapped her fingers on her bag of nuts and hummed a Katy Perry song.

When I got off the highway, I could feel the magical wards placed on the exit ramp. They were designed to repulse humans and keep them from wandering into town accidentally. A dilapidated billboard on the rural road leading into town read, "Welcome to Paradise Falls."

As I drove through town, we passed a few cars and trucks, and there were people walking down the sidewalks going about their business. But, strangely, many of the buildings had broken windows, patchy roofs, and were in serious need of fresh paint.

Tizzy had her face pressed against the passenger window. "What in ten holy hells has happened here?"

"I wish I knew." No matter how much I'd hated the place, it had been a lovely town. After the main four-way stop by the courthouse and police department, I took a left and headed south toward the shifter part of town. To Lily's house.

If the main part of town was rundown, Lily's block was ramshackle.

Tizzy nibbled on a claw. "I'm scared now, Hazel."

"We'll be fine," I told her, but I couldn't keep the nervous butterflies in my tummy still. Automatically, I patted my Glock.

Tizzy noticed. "Surrre. We'll be fine, says the lady arming herself for a homecoming."

I moved my hand away from my piece and back to the steering wheel. "Lily's the next block over."

When I parked, Tizzy rolled down the window.

"Do you mind? I want to check out the neighborhood."

"And a certain Jackie Stringer?" I gave her a wary glance. "Besides, I thought you were scared?"

"Don't be a buzzkill. Besides, you can't hurt what you can't catch."

She had a point. Tizzy was small but quick and resourceful. "Go," I told her. "Have fun."

Tizzy didn't wait for me to change my mind. She was out the window in less than a second, and all I saw was squirrel butt in my rearview mirror as she hurried down the sidewalk and out of view.

The Mason house was on Felicity, one of the many ridiculous "heavenly" names the town's forefathers had given the streets. I'd grown up on Arcadia, uber-grateful my parents hadn't bought a house on Shangri-La.

The white paint was peeled and cracked on the small two-story home, but the lawn was mowed, the windows were clean, and the porch was clutter-free. A green and yellow compact truck with a short box bed was parked in the small driveway. The dent behind the back left wheel brought back fond memories of our hell-raising days.

"Haze!" Lily shouted as she ran out her front door. She'd lost weight since high school, and even back then, she hadn't had any extra pounds to spare. Her shirt hung loose, and her jeans were held up with a belt. Her hair was still the most beautiful shade of russet red.

I looked at her truck and grinned, "I can't believe you're still driving this old beater."

"Martha is reliable." Lily put her hands on her hips and nodded to me. "Unlike someone else I could mention."

"Hey," I help up my hands. "I'm here now."

She paused a couple of feet in front of me. "Yes," she said. "You are."

This close, I could see how bloodshot her eyes were. So much so, it dimmed the vibrant green of her irises. I scooped her into my arms and squeezed her until her back popped. "I'm so sorry about Danny."

"Me too," she said, sad and sick with grief. We hugged until she patted me on the back and eased out of my embrace. "Most days, I'm okay. Knowing you were coming, re-started the waterworks." She hugged me again, quickly and briefly. "I'm really glad you're here. Maybe you can get the answers that I can't."

"I'll talk to the police chief in the morning."

"Fun, fun," she quipped.

"Yep. As fun as a root canal."

Lily gave me an incredulous look. "You've had a root canal?"

"Not hardly," I scoffed. Witches didn't suffer

from human ailments like bad teeth. Which meant I could have all the chocolate I wanted, never brush my teeth, and still have healthy, pearly whites. "But I've heard they're awful. Anyhow, I plan on talking to the chief as a courtesy."

"That'll be interesting." She gave me an appraising stare. "You know it's Dirk Nichols, right? That guy hasn't liked you since he was a patrol officer."

"You mean Dick Knuckles," I said with a groan. "Not that guy. You blow up one tiny little outhouse at a homecoming game...." I groaned at the horrifying memory. "What happened to Chief Tibbs?"

"He retired," Lily said. "And you made a hell-of-a-mess of the football field, and Nichols got put on clean-up duty to clean up the, well, doody."

I tried not to laugh. The incident had started a two-year string of traffic stops and parking tickets, all courtesy of Officer Dick.

Lily looped her arm in mine and steered me toward the house. "Since Nichols is a warlock, he has a long memory. He won't have forgotten you."

"That's probably true." Witches and warlocks didn't have perfect recall, but it was pretty darn close, which is why I hated my childhood—too many vivid details I'd like to forget. I envied the humans who could rewrite history with their memories.

I yanked my bags out of the back of my vehicle,

and Lily grabbed one, and I took the other. We rolled them up the driveway toward her house. "Nichols, huh? Well, that sucks." I hated the idea of having Nichols hold the crap-tastrophe of my most embarrassing night over my head. "In my defense, I was trying to cast a scent-hiding spell."

Like I said earlier, I'm not great with magic. Often times the simplest spells blew up in my face or, in this instance, the spell blew up on my butt.

It had been one of the few times that I'd chanced a teleport home. I'd actually made it pretty close to the target. I'd landed in a tree in our backyard. I looked and smelled like I'd been wading in a sewer. Gross.

My dad had laughed about the incident, but my mother—an ache pinched my stomach as I thought of her—she'd been so angry with me when Charlie Tibbs, the police chief at the time, knocked on our front door.

I shook my head at the painful memory before turning my attention back to Lily. "Besides, shifters have delicate noses," I said in my defense. "And I didn't want everyone to know I had to poop."

"You mean you didn't want one certain shifter to know." She giggled when I gave her a scathing glance. "You know they make something called Poo-Pourri."

"Sure, *now*." I rolled my eyes and laughed. "Let's

get my bags inside and have some coffee so we can really talk. Oh, and I also have an appointment with Adele Adams and the Witch-Shifter Coalition Council tomorrow afternoon.

She chewed her lower lip and tugged on a lock of her hair. "About that—"

Before she could finish, a bloodcurdling scream pierced the quiet street. Lily's face blanched, and sparks tickled from my fingertips.

"That's Joy Decker," Lily declared.

"Stay here," I instructed her as I drew my weapon and headed toward the scream.

John Decker, Lily's wereraccoon neighbor, ran out of his house, his wife Joy, dressed in a house gown, hot on his trail.

"Help!" he hollered. "It's Boyd. It's awful."

Joy was sobbing so hard she began to puke. "That's not my child," she heaved. "Not my Boyd. It can't be."

"Is there someone else in the house?" I asked John.

"No." He shook his head. "I don't think so."

I looked at Lily. "Call the police."

She nodded and took out her phone.

With practiced caution, I made my way up the Deckers' porch steps, through the front door with my weapon ready, and into their small home.

CHAPTER 3

JEOPARDY BLARED in the house on an old television in the living room. The rust-colored sofa had an indention on the left side. Probably Joy's spot, since the only other furniture in the room was a large brown recliner with a peeling vinyl cover. I couldn't see a woman putting her bare legs on that scratchy surface.

I cleared the front of the house and made my way down the hall. The first door on the right had to be Joy and John's bedroom. It was tidy, with the bed made. Next was a towel closet, then a bathroom. All clear. The last door at the end of the hall was Boyd's bedroom.

I had a memory flash of Lily and me, elementary age, jumping up and down on Boyd's bed while he judged who could go the highest. He'd been a goofy and funny kid. Not too bright but genuinely nice.

The wall near his door had a grease smudge. It was probably nothing, but Joy was a fairly neat housekeeper; even with the old worn furniture, the bare floor of the hall was swept, and the carpet had been vacuumed. I braced myself for what I might encounter.

The door was slightly open, so I peered inside. "Oh, Goddess." I put my hand to my mouth.

What I assumed was Boyd looked more like a twisted lump of misshapen flesh with patches of white and black fur. An arm was extended out from what looked like a double roll of fat, and the waving hand at the end of the appendage had slender black claws.

It was the most awful thing I'd ever seen, and that was saying a lot, considering my line of work.

I cast a sideways glance at the bulging monstrosity. Was this really sweet, affable Boyd? He looked as if he'd been mid-shift when things had suddenly gone very wrong. Had this been done with magic? That would have been the simplest explanation, considering Boyd's current state.

Witches and warlocks could naturally detect the use of power on people and objects. It was innate in our species. So, I stretched out my senses and searched for any hint of magic and felt none of the familiar tingles of witch power in this room.

A skittering up my leg startled me, and I stumbled forward into the room.

A high, squeaky voice said, with great alarm, "What the fudge? Goddess in a mini-skirt! That's some awful crap."

I pushed Tizzy away from my ear and farther out onto my shoulder. "Don't sneak up on me at a crime scene, Tiz. Not cool."

"I wanted to warn you that the police chief is here."

"Why warn me?" I asked.

She waved her hands excitedly. "It's Dick Knuckles."

I nodded. "I know. Lily told me."

"Why would the peckers in this town promote him to asshole-in-charge?" Tizzy made an angry tittering sound. "I overheard him talking out there. He knows you're in here, and he looks ready to blow a dozen veins in his flabby nose."

Since Nichols was a warlock, Tizzy was exaggerating his looks. He would be handsome, like most warlocks. Regrettably, Lily, Tizzy, and I might have pranked him once or twice in our misspent youth, after he started picking on me. But surely the man wouldn't hold a grudge after all these years. Besides, we were both law enforcement officers now. I hoped he'd extend me some courtesy.

"Officer Baylor," I heard Nichols say from the living room. I felt the color and heat drain from my face. *Not Ford. Not Ford. Not Ford. Please don't let it be Ford.* "Escort Miz—he said it with a really hard Z—Kinsey to the police station. If she gives you any trouble, arrest her for interfering with a potential crime scene."

"Yes, Chief." Oh, Goddess have mercy. It was definitely Ford. I recognized the low timbre of his sexy voice. It made my skin shiver.

"Crap on a cracker," I muttered.

"The po-po is coming for you, Haze."

"I *am* the po-po," I reminded Tiz.

If I was getting hauled to jail, I might as well get my money's worth. I strolled farther into the room and closer to the body, careful of where I stepped. The room smelled vaguely of the skunky tang of recreational pot. There was a pair of jeans thrown haphazardly on the floor, but otherwise, the room was as neat as the rest of the house. Boyd's lamp had a multifaceted round crystal hanging from a switch chain, and just under that was a water bong, confirming my marijuana suspicions.

While my magic wasn't strong, I'd gotten good at location and reveal spells from a *Witchcraft for Idiots* book. I'd bought it at a bookstore on a lark before Quantico, and while most of the book was nonsense, a few of the spells, with a little tweaking, had worked. It had been a valuable tool when I started working kidnappings. The spells helped me to discern actual clues from normal items at a crime scene.

My time was limited, so I quickly incanted:

"Goddess bring me second sight.

Turn the darkness into light.

A deed is done, most obscene.

Reveal the path, unseen seen.

Done is done, Goddess grant to me,

Second sight, so mote it be."

It wasn't Shakespeare, but it did the trick. I scanned the room again. The dangling crystal lit up like a glow stick, marking it as important. The bong stayed muted. Guess the pot wasn't the culprit. The side of his dresser glowed as well. I walked over for a closer look. A rough capital *H* had been carved into the wood.

Why was it glowing? Maybe Boyd had tried to scratch out his killer's name.

Only one more spot in the room glowed. It was on the headboard behind the Boyd blob. I steeled my courage and forced my feet to move me in that direction. On the wall was another greasy smudge.

I leaned in close to see if it had an odor, but an overpowering aroma of cinnamon flooded the room. "What the heck?"

Then I heard the voice again. "Ms. Kinsey, I'm gonna need you to come out of here." The powerful scent of the man, like a strong cup of chai tea, wafted, making me hungry and horny. I braced my jittery-floppity stomach, then turned my head to meet his gaze.

And there he was. Ford Baylor. All six-foot-nine-inches of tall, dark, and bear. His chocolate hair, the color of molten lava cake, was cut short and neat instead of the mop of thick curls he wore in high school. And the short, well-groomed beard was different as well. Light blue eyes framed by thick dark lashes gazed at me from across the room.

My girly bits sang soprano as our gazes met. It should be a sin to be that handsome. I gulped, looking for the nearest window to jump out. How crappy was it that Ford could still make my heart race? I glued my feet to the floor to keep from running over there to sniff him like a freshly baked cinnamon roll. The last thing I needed was the distraction of a man I couldn't have.

There's a lump of raccoon shifter in this room, I reminded myself. *This is a crime scene for the love of inappropriate behavior, not a class reunion, so get ahold of yourself!*

"Hey," I crooned because I'm such a smooth talker.

Ford raised a brow as if to ask if I was going to give him grief or not. Other than that, it didn't seem like he recognized me at all. I'm ashamed of how disappointed I felt.

I reached into my back pocket and pulled out my wallet. "Special Agent Kinsey," I said. When I flashed him the badge, he didn't seem all that impressed.

"Special Agent Kinsey," he acknowledged. "I'm going to need you to come down to the station with me. Chief's orders."

I grimaced. "This is ridiculous."

"I don't want to have to arrest you." Officer Baylor took out his handcuffs, and on another occasion, I might have smiled, because, well, handcuffs, but his cold attitude was pissing me off.

"Police brutality!" Tizzy trilled. She crawled down my back, her tiny nails scratching me on the way down.

"Ow." I squirmed when she clung to my jeans on the backside of my thigh. I was looking sooo not cool in front of the one person I wanted to look cool for. I glared down at the squirrel; her head poked out from around my ass, and her tail swished against the back of my thigh. "Tizzy," I ordered. "Out."

"But Haze—" she protested.

"Nope." I cut off her argument. "Go be with Lily. I got this."

She looked up at Ford and glared, her long eyelashes fluttering with anger. "If you hurt Hazel, I swear I'll hunt you down and harvest your nuts."

His eyes widened, and he cast the briefest of glances at his crotch before meeting my familiar's hot gaze. "Duly noted."

She harrumphed loudly, and it sounded more like someone stepped on a dog toy. "I have my eyes on you, Grizzly Adams." With two fingers, she pointed at her eyes and up to his and back to hers. "Watch your back." After her final warning, she ran between Ford's legs and out of the room.

"She's intense," he said.

I blew out a breath. "You're not kidding."

He jangled his cuffs. "The easy way or the hard way, Kinsey."

"Are you really going to be a douche about this?"

"That's Officer Douche."

He was not going to let up or let me go, so I nodded. "Fine. The easy way. For now."

The Paradise Falls Police Station hadn't changed too much on the outside over the past fifteen years, and the inside was just as underwhelming. We were let inside the locked door by Officer Givens, a plump but pleasant woman dressed in full uniform. The air inside was stale, and I felt a little claustrophobic. It was, after all, the nightmare of my childhood, thanks to Dirk Nichols. The chief, at the time, had been

Charlie Tibbs, a good old boy werebadger with a badge. He was the only reason I'd managed to get out of Paradise Falls with a clean record. The way the police were handling Danny's murder told me the town was worse off without him.

I wanted to ask Ford why he smelled so much like a streusel topping all the time, but instead, I asked, "Why has the investigation stalled on Danny Mason?"

His cheeks reddened for a moment, but he didn't answer.

"Is it true every bone was broken in his body?"

"I'm not allowed to discuss an open investigation."

"Is it, though? An open investigation?" Yes, I was pushing buttons, but I needed more information on the case, and maybe I could goad him into saying something that might help me help Lily. Either that, or I was upset he didn't seem to recognize me at all. "What happened to him was more than a troubled young man getting what was coming to him? I know Danny wasn't a peach, but damn, he didn't deserve this."

Ford's gaze connected with mine. "Why did you come back here, Hazel?"

"Oh." I crossed my arms. "You do remember me then."

The spicy scent of him grew stronger as his gaze

briefly met mine. He pulled out a chair and gestured for me to sit near a small desk. He took the seat in front where an old computer took up space.

"I remember you." He typed into the keyboard. A beep sounded. The screen came up with a brown-and-white scheme. "Full name."

"This is dumb."

"Is that a legal name change, or just something you like to go by?" I saw the hint of a smile curl the corner of his mouth.

So he wasn't a complete robot. "Hazel Marie Kinsey," I answered.

"Date of birth."

"Old enough."

"Date of birth," he repeated.

"I'm an agent with the FBI," I told him, "not a criminal, and I don't like being treated like one."

"This is a witness statement. Not a criminal report."

"Not the point."

"Kinda is."

"Fine." I slouched in a pouty huff...then remembered the card the Grand Inquisitor had given me. I grabbed my wallet, pulled out the little white rectangle that said "pass" and slid it across the desk.

Ford growled. "I'll let the chief know when he gets back from the crime scene. Until then, make yourself comfortable."

I smirked. "I'll do that."

Three hours, two vending machine vanilla cakes with pink frosting, and one bad cup of coffee later, Chief Nichols ushered me into his office. "I don't like this one damn bit, Mizz Kinsey. This is my town. I really ought to throw you out on your butt."

I curled my lip. "Did you talk to the Grand Inquisitor?"

His blanching cheeks told me he had. "You should have checked in with me the minute you hit town."

"I was planning on it first thing in the morning. How in the heck was I supposed to know Lily Mason's neighbor was going to die?" I didn't add "in a gruesome, most horrifying and awful way." I think that part was implied.

"Can't be helped now," he blustered. "Being related to Clementine Battles will get you no special favors here, Kinsey." Anger wrinkled his forehead, marring his unlined face. He wasn't ugly. But, even so, past his full head of blond hair and symmetrical features, there was nothing appealing about the man. He was the kind of guy who wore his warts on the inside. "It didn't save your father from prison," he added, "and it damn sure won't save you if you get in my way."

My anger matched his, but I used my training to appear stoic and unruffled. "I need all the investigation files and notes you have on Daniel Mason." I resisted calling him Dick. He might be under orders to cooperate, but I was certain he planned to make things difficult for me.

His expression soured even more. "I'll have Officer Baylor get you whatever files you require, but nothing leaves this station. You understand me?"

"Perfectly."

He grunted. "As long as we're clear."

"Crystal," I told him.

"You're still an asshole," he said.

"Ditto that, Chief."

His lips thinned out as he frowned. "Is there anything else I can help you with, Mizzz Kinsey?"

I didn't bother to correct him with a "Special Agent" comeback. I simply said, "Nope. The files are good for now."

"Then get the hell out of my office."

I stood up, turned on my heel, and did as I was told.

On the way out, I saw John and Joy Decker clinging to each other in the hall outside. A man with black hair and a salt-and-pepper beard sat with them. He murmured quiet comforts to the grieving parents. John looked up at me, his brown eyes glistening with tears.

"I'm so sorry, Mr. and Mrs. Decker," I said with sympathy.

Joy sobbed harder, but John tightened his mouth and nodded. "Thank you, Hazel."

"Hazel Kinsey?" The man next to them stood up and held out his hand. "I'm Robert Townsend, a good friend of the Deckers. If I can do anything to aid you in your investigation, let me know."

How did he know I was investigating?

I could feel the power in his grip as he shook my hand. "I'm the alpha of the *paullulum mammalia.*"

I'll admit that I wasn't well-versed in shifter hierarchy. Lily and I rarely talked about the differences between witches and therianthropes. We knew how to make each other laugh, and we always had each other's backs. Even so, I wouldn't know a *paullulum* from a pole dance. "I apologize, but I'm not familiar with the term," I said to Townsend.

"It encompasses all the small animal shifters," he explained.

Ah. He was the head mucky-muck over the chipmunk, beaver, badger, rabbit, and raccoon shifters in the area. Which meant he was part of the Witch-Shifter council. He would've been apprised of my arrival. "I appreciate your cooperation, sir."

He gave me a smile that both reflected friendliness and proper decorum for the mood in the hall.

To the Deckers, I said, "I'll be at Lily's house for the next week or so. If you all need anything, please let me know."

CHAPTER 4

THE SPARSELY FURNISHED guest bedroom at Lily's consisted of a full-size bed with a worn but clean quilt. The colorful blanket made of l and sage green blocks had belonged to Lily's great-great-grandmother. It had been handed down from one daughter to the next until Lily's mom was presented with it on her wedding day. Now that her mom was dead, Lily had become its keeper. I envied her the cozy history of a loving family, something I'd never really experienced. My mother had been a cold woman.

The rest of the room had been designed for utility. There was an ironing board in the corner. Several large, green storage tubs—the kind you can pick up at the general store—were stacked near the closet. The vanity had an oval mirror that had lost a distracting amount of silvering.

I sat on the edge of the bed staring at Danny's

slim police file. Despite Nichols' order, I'd snuck it out of the police station. Screw Dick and his attitude about me and my investigation. Besides, it had been difficult to concentrate with Ford's scent covering every inch of the place. As I read through the limited investigation, the thing that angered me the most was how little had been done to find Danny's killer. It made me want to punch someone in the throat.

I rolled over on the mattress and combed through what information the police had gathered. Next, I jotted down a few key details and photographed anything else I thought important. The crime scene report had been written by Dennis Mitchel. He'd been the lead detective on the case. I'd asked for a meeting with him, but Ford had told me he'd taken a leave of absence for a family emergency. Bad for me. Good for Mitchel. I wanted to grill his nards over an open flame. There were more holes in this investigation than a colander.

The report said that Danny's body was found in a folded heap in an abandoned barn out on the edge of town. The property had gone into foreclosure five years earlier and was currently owned by the bank. Very little blood had been found at the scene other than a small amount that had dried around Danny's mouth. His face had been as bloated and purple as the rest of his body. Unidentifiable.

If it hadn't been for the wallet in his pocket that

contained his driver's license, it would've taken much longer to identify him. Along with the license, his wallet contained a Paradise Falls Grocer card, a family picture of him and Lily with their parents when he was five years old, and seven dollars in ones.

The toxicology report showed trace evidence of ketamine, barely enough to even effect a shifter. The autopsy report confirmed what Lily had told me. Every bone in Danny's body had been broken. Not a single one had been missed, from the individual plates in his skull down to the tips of his toes. Even the tiny bones inside his ears had been cracked. No wonder he'd been unrecognizable in the crime scene photos.

I felt sick while reading about the 205 bones broken before the rib fracture that punctured his heart. Who or what could've done that? Be so precise? And how long had they made Danny suffer?

I shuddered, pushing the thought to the back of my mind.

Other than his body, no other material evidence had been found. No fingerprints, stray hairs, or fibers. There had been no footprints at the scene either. Someone had managed to kill Danny and dump his body in a dirt-floor barn without leaving even the tiniest scuff mark behind.

I had to stop thinking of the victim as Danny. I

had to put my emotions aside if I wanted to be the person Lily needed me to be, but the more I read about the case, the harder it was to stay dispassionate.

Lily's gentle knock on the door had me closing my notes fast and shoving them and the police file under the pillow. She cracked the door open.

"Hey," she said, her eyes red with exhaustion. "Can I come in?"

"Of course," I said a little too brightly. "It's been a rough day, huh?"

"Rough year," she amended.

I was an idiot. "Gosh, I'm sorry, Lils. I didn't mean—"

Her simple smile let me off the hook. "I've missed you. I'm so glad you're here." She leaned forward, and her smile grew wider. "I can't believe Dick Knuckles had you hauled down to the station. What a butt-wipe."

"No kidding." I patted the bed as an invitation for her to sit next to me. "And who the hell does Officer Baylor think he is, threatening to cuff me? I'm a federal agent, for the love of Pete."

"You mean Officer Woo-woo, don't you?" Her smile verged on a grin now as she took the offer. "Or at least that's what you called him in high school. Ford "Woo-woo" Baylor, because every time you saw him, you'd say woo-woo."

A hot flush crept to my cheeks. "I'm not having this conversation."

"Woooo-woo," she teased. "You pined for that boy like nobody's business our senior year."

"Because it *was* nobody's business," I countered. I had to admit, I was glad to see Lily having fun, even if it was at my expense. I smirked. "I crushed on him hardcore, didn't I?"

"Uhm, if by hardcore you mean writing Mrs. Haze Baylor all over your spiral notebooks and tennis shoes every day, then yes, I'll agree, you crushed on him hardcore."

"I hate you."

"You're a detective." Lily spread her hands wide. "The evidence speaks for itself."

I laughed. She wasn't wrong. I think there were a few textbooks I'd graffitied as well. Ford had been, as my teenage self would have said, dreamy. Nothing had changed in that department. He still looked and smelled better than any man I'd ever met.

"I'm sure he's happily married with a dozen cubs by now." I frowned at the unhappy thought.

"You know therians actually have babies, right?"

"Whatever." I rolled my eyes. "Did he marry Greta Sharp?" She'd been a bear shifter like Ford, and the two of them had been Prom King and Queen our senior year.

"He didn't mate with Greta."

"Then who?"

Lily grinned. "He's single."

A wave of adrenaline rushed through me, raising gooseflesh on my skin. "You're kidding, right?"

"Nope. I hear about him dating occasionally, but nothing has stuck." She gave me a meaningful look, which I poo-pooed away.

"He barely remembered me from high school, Lily. Besides, I've moved on with my life."

"I can see that by the ring on your finger and your phone gallery full of pictures of your children."

"Smart-ass."

"Smart cougar," she corrected. "The ass shifters live in another part of town."

We fell into a fit of laughter verging on hysteria. Frankly, it was better than crying our eyes out. After a few minutes, we settled down. Lily reclined on the bed next to me, both of us staring at the flaking popcorn ceiling.

"I used to love coming here," I told her. "It was my favorite place in Paradise Falls." I turned my head and looked at her. "Amend that. Anywhere we could hang out together was my favorite place to be."

"Same here," she told me. Her voice was quiet as she asked, "What happened to Boyd? The morgue guys rolled out something large and lumpy in a black zipped-up bag. It didn't look like a person was in there."

The horrific image of Boyd waving at me with black claws popped into my head. I shuddered. "It didn't look much like a person out of the bag, either."

"How awful."

"Did Danny and Boyd hang out?"

"Do you think the two deaths are related?"

"No. Maybe. I don't know." The two deaths were months apart, but the unusual circumstances of both cases made me wonder. "I'll have to wait and see what Boyd's autopsy shows. The only two things both of them have in common is the bizarre, unexplained nature. I mean, Boyd looked like something out of a D horror movie."

"Magic or was it a physical attack?" she asked.

I shook my head. "It looked like something only witch magic could do. However, I didn't feel any residual magic in the room or on the victim."

She cast me a wary glance that made my heart hurt. "Are you sure?"

"I cross my heart, Lily." I touched her hand. "Do you think Danny's death was caused by a spell?"

She shrugged, her green eyes sparkling with unshed tears. "I don't know. I thought maybe...but the medical examiner had said no. It all felt like someone was trying to cover something up."

"I don't blame you for being suspicious. I thought

Boyd's death was magical as well, which is why I checked. But honest, Lils, I felt nothing."

"Well, you always say you're a terrible witch. Can you be wrong?"

I forced a smile because I knew she was only half teasing about the terrible witch comment. "Not in this case. I may not be any good at spellcasting and such, but it's innate in my kind to be able to feel our kind of magic. And there is no spell that can block it because we'd feel the blocking spell."

She nodded. "And was Boyd like… Was he broken like Danny?"

"No." I shuddered as I thought about Boyd's misshapen form. "If I hadn't seen him for myself—like, if I'd seen it in a picture or on the computer—I would have thought he was photoshopped. I'd never seen anything so awful."

"Tell me."

"I don't know, Lils. It's kind of terrible."

"I'm not a delicate flower, Haze. No matter what my parents named me."

That's my Lily, I thought. She might only be a tiny five feet two inches, but she was always the stronger one between the two of us. I'd relied on her strength so many times when we were young. Then her parents died.

Shame filled me. I'd left her behind. I had been so

caught up in my own drama with my mother's death, and my father being hauled off to jail for her murder. Before his mother had come to take him away, he'd told me to leave Paradise Falls as soon as I could, and I did. I couldn't run soon enough or fast enough for my taste. And over the years, I'd rarely looked back.

"Come on, Hazel," Lily said. "I need to know."

I sighed. "Okay, I'm not sure how to describe it though. Uhm, have you ever heard of those weird twin tumors, where they find big lumps of flesh with teeth and hair and other gross stuff inside someone?"

"I'm pretty sure that's called a teratoma."

Her knowledge of the term reminded me that she'd wanted to go to medical school. Her parents' deaths had sure sent her down a different path. It was amazing how family crisis and drama could turn a life around.

"A teratoma, yes. So, you know what I'm talking about."

"Yes."

"Well, that's what Boyd looked like, only person-sized and with skin." I didn't mention the arm hanging out of his backside. "It was as if someone made him a twisted pretzel inside his own skin."

"You're right," Lily said. "It's terrible. That sounds as bizarre as what happened to Danny." She tapped me on the shoulder with the back of her hand. "What can do that, if not witch magic? I mean, shifters are strong, but I don't know if they have the finesse to do all this."

"I don't know, Lily. Not yet. But whatever it is, it's evil, Lils. And real evil has a steep price tag. Magic or not, I'm not ruling out witches. It may not be witchcraft, but something unnatural or supernatural did that to Boyd and possibly to Danny."

"If it is witches, what can you do?"

"I have the Grand Inquisitor's blessing to investigate, but I'm not sure I'm equipped to deal with a powerful witch. I have a gun, but someone strong could spell it away with a few words. And as you already said, I'm a terrible witch. My magic seems to always backfire on me."

"You mean like when you accidentally knocked yourself out when you sent a current of electricity into your locker, and it backfired on you."

I gave her a sour look. "Yes. Like that."

She giggled.

My cell phone rang, saving me from having her provide me with several more examples of my ineptitude. The number was "Unknown." I answered, "Special Agent Kinsey," out of habit.

"This is Officer Baylor," a deep, sexy voice said on the other end. My stomach dropped, and my palms began to sweat. "Can we meet for coffee?"

"Uhm…"

Lily's eyes widened as she mouthed the word "yes."

"Yes," I said. "Sure."

"Lolo's Diner on Elysium Street in an hour?"

Lily nodded at me emphatically. I glared at her. "I'll be there," I told Ford. "With bells on." I disconnected the call, kicking myself for the last part. I looked at Lily. "With bells on? Seriously? Why the hell did I say that for?"

"Because you looo-ooove him," she crooned. "Love makes you stupid."

"You're stupid," I told her as I devolved into my fifteen-year-old self again. "I don't love him."

"Of course not, Mrs. Haze Baylor." Lily leaped from the bed and grabbed my suitcase. "Now let's find you something to wear."

"This isn't a date."

"You don't know what it is." She threw a black dress at me. "Hope for the best, but prepare for the worst."

"I hate it when you throw my words back in my face."

Her mouth quirked up at the corner. "I know."

Tizzy rushed into the room. "I love Lolo's," she said. "Hurry up and dress so we can go."

I narrowed my gaze at my familiar. "You can't come, Tiz. This is a work meeting." A part of me hoped it was more, but Ford had said Officer Baylor, which seemed to scream work and not pleasure. "You stay here and catch up with Lily."

"I've seen Officer Baylor, Haze. You need the backup," she whined. "What if he decides to haul your butt to jail again?"

"He's not going to take me to jail." Really, I think Tiz just wanted to eavesdrop. I couldn't blame her. I'd taken her out of a paranormal town to live in a human city, which meant she'd only had me to talk to for nearly two decades. Seeing how excited and alive she'd become since we'd returned to Paradise Falls made me feel like the most selfish witch on the planet.

She'd never once complained about being alone, so foolishly, I had believed she wasn't lonely.

"Why don't you invite Jackie over? Or go to her place."

"She's mated," Tiz said, disappointment lowering her voice to an alto-soprano.

"I'm sorry."

The squirrel brightened. "I think there's a shifter shindig on Eden's Road. I might head out there if you don't mind."

I raised a suspicious brow. I'd been to a couple parties out there during my teenage years. We used to call the area the "garden of delights." Lots of booze. Lots of drugs. My head hurt just thinking about those Sunday-morning hangovers. "Those can get a little rough."

"Puh-leeeeeeaze, Haze." She clasped her tiny hands in front of her and batted her lashes. "I'm just so...sad...about Jackie. I think a party would do me some good."

Lily, who'd been listening quietly, stepped in. "I'll go with her."

"You sure?"

"Yep," she said, laughing as Tizzy climbed her leg and arm until she landed on Lily's shoulder. "It's been a long time since I've gotten out of this old house. It'll do me good."

"Okay," I said. "Tiz, Lily's in charge."

"Haze!"

I narrowed my gaze.

She threw up her manicured paws. "Fine. Lily's in charge."

CHAPTER 5

LOLO'S DINER looked straight out of a movie from the nineteen-fifties. It was red and white on the outside and lit up with bright neon signage advertising shakes, burgers, and fries. Oh, Lord have mercy, I could smell the burgers. The delicious scent took me back to when Lily and I would sit in her dad's old Coup and people watch safely from our own private bubble.

Ford Baylor stood near the entrance. He wore a dark blue T-shirt that stretched taut across his broad chest, and a pair of jeans that hugged his thickly muscular thighs. I wiped the drool from the corner of my mouth. He was chatting away with a woman who had wavy strawberry-blonde hair and wore a tight cardigan and a ruffle skirt, so he didn't seem to notice my arrival.

I groaned when the woman turned my direction, and I got a good look at her face. Tanya Gellar. Ugh. She had been one of the popular girls in school. A talented witch, class president, star on the softball team, gorgeous, and mean as a snake.

I almost put the car in reverse, because, as much as I'd like to rewrite history, I was not what you'd call one of the popular kids in school. I wasn't witchy enough for the witches or the popular shifters. People like Tanya had made my formative years intolerable. The fact that she had been best friends with Ford's girlfriend Greta played no part in my dislike of her.

I am a freaking FBI agent. I am tough, and I carry a gun. I put away my teenage angst and got out of the car. When Ford saw me, he waved. Tanya gave me resting bitch face, which I assumed was her way of saying, "Howdy, neighbor."

"You're late," Ford said. His furrowed brow and deep frown made me squirm, and my teenage angst returned with a vengeance. Tanya glared in my direction but didn't comment.

My jealousy got the better of me. "It looks like you found a way to occupy your time," I told him.

His face flushed. "Dr. Gellar is the medical examiner. I thought you might want to hear her initial report on Boyd Decker."

"Oh." Color me petty. I had to find a way to put

my weirdly strong feelings for Ford aside so I could concentrate on why I was back in Paradise Falls. "Yeah, actually, that would be great. Did you do the autopsy on Danny Mason as well?"

"Yes," Tanya said. "That was…unsettling. As unsettling as my findings about Decker."

I gave her a nod and polite smile, the one I had perfected after years of working with local law enforcement. "I appreciate you taking time out of your schedule, Dr. Gellar."

She sniffed. "You can thank Ford." She smiled. "I mean Officer Baylor."

Ugh, kill me now. In my estimation, her little slip was her way of letting me know that the relationship between Ford and her was more than professional.

She looked at him and flashed a flirty smile, confirming my suspicions. "I owe him a favor or two." She turned up her nose at me. "Never thought he'd waste his marker on this, though."

What she meant was she never thought he'd waste the favor on me. Funny enough, that revelation improved my mood.

Ford's frown deepened. "Let's go inside," he said. "We can discuss this over pie and coffee."

I forced a smile. "Sounds good." His cinnamon scent had me jonesing for apple pie.

The place was only half full, which was sad for a Friday night. When I was in high school, Lolo's was always jumping with business. The back booth on the right side had been where Lily and I spent many a weeknight plotting world domination over a malted milkshake.

I followed Ford and Tanya to an open booth near the restrooms. Tanya slid in on Ford's side of the table, and my heart sank a little. Why did this guy always get under my skin? Even after the years I'd spent away from Paradise Falls, I couldn't get him out of my head. I had compared every man I'd ever dated to Ford, and none of them had measured up.

A young waitress with flawless skin and bouncy, shiny hair and a name badge that said "Becksy" took our orders. Probably a teenage witch. She was a little too put together, as if someone was dipping into a spell book. Besides, no self-respecting shifter would name their child Becksy. It was silly and pretentious. Our kind could get that way sometimes. It was the same machinations that made rich folks call their kids Biff or Mitsy or Scooter.

"What do you have on Decker?" I asked, getting straight to the point.

"I only have preliminary exam results. Some of the tests will take several days, some even weeks to draw any real conclusions," Tanya said.

"What can you tell me then?"

Before Tanya could answer, Becksy came back to our table with three pieces of apple pie, three coffee cups, and a carafe. She put the pie down and then the cups, which she filled with steaming-hot java.

"Sugar and cream are there." She pointed to a silver condiments caddy near the window on our table. "Let me know if I can get you anything else." She paid good attention to detail, and her smile was amiable. I decided Becksy had more going for her than a pretty face.

When she left us, I turned back to Tanya again. "What do you know?" I took a bite of the pie and resisted making *mmmm-mmmm* noises as I chewed the little slice of Heaven.

"A rapid toxicology screen showed opiates in his blood, but not enough to overdose him. It was more of a recreational dose. I haven't counted all the broken bones yet, but much like Daniel Mason, I think all of Boyd's have been fractured in one way or another." She pressed on clinically. "It's my belief he was mid-shift when…the homicide occurred." Her eyes widened for a moment at the memory.

"What was the COD?"

"Cause of death was a rib to the heart."

"Like Danny."

"Just like," Tanya agreed.

"Didn't Danny have drugs in his system too?" I was so focused on my own dessert, it surprised me to see Tanya had already eaten most of hers, and Ford's had completely disappeared from his plate. At least I could pretend the cinnamon I was smelling was from the food and not from the sexy furball sitting directly across the table from me.

"Same as Boyd. Recreational amounts only."

Shifters burned through drugs quick, but I knew from some high school experimentation that Lily and I had partaken in occasionally that marijuana had a long-lasting calming effect on the two-natured. Lily had been buzzed for hours. The opiates would have been a quick burn, though. Strange that Boyd and Danny both had them in their system at the time of death.

"Any trace evidence?" I asked. "DNA under the fingernails, a stray hair, saliva, anything?"

"Nothing so far," Tanya said. "I'm going to examine the body again tomorrow. And I'll have the lab results for a more detailed tox screen in two days."

"Will you keep me informed?"

"I'll keep Ford informed," she said. She slid from the seat and placed her hand on Ford's shoulder. She gazed down at him, a sweet smile on her lips. "I'll talk to you tomorrow?" She turned the statement into a question.

"Sure enough." He gave her a quick smile. "Thanks, Tanya."

"Anytime for you. You know that." Her wide smile made me want to throttle myself for caring.

When she put a ten-dollar bill on the table, Ford shook his head. "On me."

She nodded and took the money back. "Next time, I'll buy."

Ford smiled at her, and I wanted to lunge across the table and beat the crap out of both of them. "You're on."

Did they just make a date? Right in front of me? Was I freaking invisible? Outwardly, I maintained my cool. "Yeah, thanks for the help, Dr. Gellar. See you around."

She gave me a tight-lipped smile that basically said, "Not if I see you first."

What-evs. Once she left, the tension inside me eased. "Thanks for that," I told Ford.

He hadn't had to share information about Boyd Decker. It wasn't the case the Grand Inquisitor gave me permission to investigate, but I was pretty sure the two were connected.

He shrugged. "There is nothing against the rules that three high school friends can't get together for a bite to eat."

Was he trying to tell me something? Like maybe Lily was right, and there was a massive cover-up going on surrounding her brother's death? "Why isn't there more information about Danny's death? The investigation is amateurish and, frankly, an embarrassment to the community. There are no suspects or witness statements. No follow-up reports. The officer in charge, Dennis Mitchell, is either a complete incompetent or he is complicit. Do you know what emergency took him out of town? I'd really like to speak to him."

Ford looked at me with a bland expression on his face and remained silent.

"Who is tying your hands, Ford?"

"How's life in Kansas City?" he asked. "I hear you're posted there now."

"In town for less than five minutes, and the word about me is already getting around."

He narrowed his gaze on me, his blue eyes withering me with their intensity. "I heard about it two years ago when you were first posted there."

"Seriously?" His delicious scent grew more intense. "You didn't even act like you knew who I was earlier. Or do you just get the 9-1-1 on all the ex-residents in town?"

"Don't pretend like you don't know."

"Know what?" I'd never been so confused in my life, not even when my college roommate got drunk and kissed me in the communal bathroom.

Ford honest-to-goodness growled. "I do when that ex-resident is my mate."

"Huh? Wait. What?" You could have surprised me less if a piano had suddenly fallen out of the sky and dropped on my head. "Mate? Like a friend?

Compadre? Buddy? I don't think we were ever any of those things." Though it didn't mean I wouldn't have liked it to be so.

"Don't be dense, Hazel."

Maybe I *was* dense, because I just didn't get what he was talking about or why he was so angry with me. "I…" Was at a loss for words. "I think I need a translator. I don't speak nonsense."

"Do you remember the night of Woolsey's party, the one out on Eden's Road at the end of our senior year?"

"Sorta." Truth be told, I'd had a lot to drink that night. "I remember waking up the next day with a hangover that lasted until graduation."

He steepled his fingers and peered over the tips at me. "So you don't remember kissing me?"

"Uhm, no." Nooooooo! It wasn't possible. I couldn't have kissed him and not remembered. This was turning into a cautionary tale about drinking and kissing for lovesick teenagers everywhere. "Was it good?" It must have been, right, for him to remember all these years later.

"Actually, it was awful. Abrupt. Sloppy," Ford said. "But your scent took me over." He sniffed the air as if he could still smell it. "Vanilla and rum."

"That was probably the booze," I murmured, mortified by this conversation. However, I'd been drinking peach schnapps and orange soda, a spin on the Fuzzy Navel that Lily and I called a Hairy Belly-button, not vanilla rum.

"Now," Ford said, "your scent is all I can think about."

"I still don't understand," I told him.

"You were best friends with a therianthrope for most of your life, Hazel, and you've never heard of mating scent?"

"We never talked about the things that made us different," I told him honestly. "We talked about our hopes and dreams of escaping Paradise Falls." And about boys and mean girls and momma drama. "We didn't talk about mating scents. I've never even heard of such a thing."

"Why doesn't this surprise me," he said. "Well, let me educate you." He stood up, all sexy six-foot-nine inches of him, and slid into the booth next to me. He smelled my hair, and I nearly peed my pants. "The scent is unique to each mated pair. For every shifter, there is only one mate. Some never find a true mate, but still marry because of genuine fondness. But when the scent happens, our inner animal is triggered by the other person, and it makes having other relationships difficult. You triggered my bear with that drunken kiss."

"Why would your bear want me?" I gulped. "I'm a witch. Besides, you didn't even know I existed in high school."

"Until that night."

"You had a girlfriend. You were with Greta."

"But we'd never triggered the mating scent in each other. We broke up shortly after graduation."

"I always thought you two would get married."

"We could have," Ford said. "But I knew I could never make her happy. Not in the way she deserved."

"Why?"

"Because she wasn't my mate. You are."

"Oh." I consider myself a smart cookie. Quick on the uptake, but I was having a hell of a time digesting and processing this conversation. "We aren't mates."

"Yes," Ford said. "We are."

"I'm not a shifter. I have no animal to trigger."

"I don't understand that part either, but you do still smell my scent, right?" He leaned to my ear, his hot breath warming my cheek. "You think about it all the time, don't you?"

He wasn't wrong. A thrill zipped through me as cinnamon filled my senses. Still, I opened my mouth to rebut him, but my phone rang, saving me from having to make words. "Kinsey here," I said without even checking out the caller's name.

"Haze," Lily shouted. I could hear music and yelling in the background. "I think you better come out to Eden's Road. Tiz is in trouble."

I didn't even hesitate. "On my way." I clicked the

phone off and looked at Ford, swallowing the lump in my throat as his sparkly blue eyes hypnotized me. "I have to go now."

"I'll drive," he said, standing up.

"Fine."

CHAPTER 6

THE DRIVE OUT to Eden's Road was intensely quiet. I didn't know how to respond to Ford's revelation. Had he really not married or mated or whatever because of me?

"I hope Tizzy is okay," I said, because it was a safe subject.

Ford gripped his steering wheel tightly. "Are we really not going to talk about what happened between us in high school?"

"Nothing happened between us in high school," I finally said.

"That's not completely true."

"I'm a witch."

"Yep," he said.

"You're a bear shifter."

"You aren't wrong about that, either."

"How is this possible?"

He shook his head. "Do you think I know? I'd heard it was possible. My mother told me that sometimes mating is a bond between two halves of one soul, and it doesn't always follow the rules."

"You told her about us?"

He shifted uncomfortably. "Not exactly, but it doesn't mean I didn't ask a question about cross-mating with witches. She said it's so rare it's almost unheard of, but rare doesn't mean never. Unless you have a better explanation for it."

A teenage witch's lovesick angst gone wrong, maybe? I didn't say it out loud. Instead, I shook my head. "We come from two different worlds," I told him. "It would never work." It didn't stop me from wanting to climb him like Mt. Everest and enjoy the view from the highest peak. But like Mt. Everest, the chance of me surviving the climb was slim. He was one big boy…er…man.

Ford nodded solemnly. "I have made my peace with being alone."

My chest squeezed. Why did I feel so guilty? It wasn't my fault he thought I was his mate. Hell, I'd been an awkward, nerdy witch during my teen years, better with math and science than witchcraft. I couldn't have magicked a pimple away, let alone cast an accidental love spell. How in the world had this happened?

As we pulled up to the party, there were at least

twenty cars lining the gravel road on both sides, three kegs sat in the open field, along with metal tubs full of ice and harder alcohol. I spotted Lily near an organized group. She jumped in the air with her hand up and gave me the "hurry up" wave.

I looked at the rowdy crowd and back to Ford. "I hope you brought your gun."

When I got to Lily, she pointed at the spectacle at the center of the crowd.

Tizzy was circling a beaver, and he was making all kinds of hissing and growling noises at her. She kept dancing around like a prize fighter, jumping and moving every time the beaver tried to whack her with his tail.

A woman, wearing an inside-out red sweater, faded blue jeans, smeared coral lipstick, and a frantic look on her face, kept yelling, "Leave her alone, Frank. It meant nothing. It was nothing. Just some harmless fun."

Goddess, Tizzy. What the hell had my familiar done now?

Lily quickly said, "Tizzy was doing shots with Colleen, and for a five-pound animal, she was holding her own, let me tell you. Then Tizzy told Colleen she was the most beautiful woman she'd ever laid eyes on, and that she'd always wanted to kiss a beaver, which I thought was funny at the time, but the next thing I knew, Colleen had shifted, and she and Tizzy were rolling around in the grass."

"Then Frank showed up."

Lily nodded. "Yep. Then Frank showed up." Her expression was aghast. "I tried to stop it, Haze. I really did, but you have no idea how hard it is to get between a squirrel and her beaver." She giggled.

I think my BFF had been doing shots as well. "Tiz!" I shouted. The squirrel snapped her gaze to me, which gave Frank the Beaver the opening he needed. His flat tail whacked Tizzy upside her little squirrel head and threw her a couple feet.

"Hey!" Ford yelled. The crowd parted for him. I think they were just excited that someone else was joining the fight. "Break it up," he said. "I'd hate to have to run you all downtown on a Friday night. Judge don't arraign any cases until Monday. It'd be a shame to screw up your entire weekend."

People backed up. But Frank Leggert, that jealous little rodent, would not be deterred. He lunged at Tizzy, who was still dazed from the smack.

"No," I yelled. "Leave her alone." I grabbed at his back, his fur slick and really hard to get any kind of hold on. He squirmed away from me, but not before I slammed a boot on his ass.

He shifted back to human, a sorry excuse for a man, naked and nursing a bruised ego and butt. "That really hurt, you stupid witch." He stood up, posturing like he was going to do something about it, but suddenly backed down. "Keep that rat away from my girl," he said then turned his venom on Lily. "Unless you all want to end up like Danny."

Before I could zap his stupid mouth, too, he hurried off after the rest of the group.

I stomped my foot and threw my hands up in victory. "That's right, douchenozzle. Run!"

Lily shook her head and pointed a finger at something behind me. I turned around to see a very imposing Ford standing with his arms crossed and his eyes trained on the running man. Well, I guess I knew why Frank had a change of heart about coming at me.

"I had it covered," I said.

Ford grunted. "Uh huh."

A pitiful squeak shifted my focus from the hulking hunk. "Oh, Tiz!" I made my way to the fallen squirrel and picked her up. "Speak to me, Tiz. Tell me you're okay." I shook her tiny chest.

She heaved a sigh, a large feral grin forming on her face. "I like beaver," she said. "A whole lot."

I rolled my eyes and looked at Lily, then at Ford. "She's fine." Still, I cradled her in my arms just in case.

My drunken best friend shook her head, remorse in her bloodshot eyes. "Gosh, Haze. I really am sorry. It all just happened so fast."

"She's starved for company," I admitted, effectively letting Lily off the hook. "I don't know if a brick wall could have stopped her."

"Hey, Ford," Lily said shyly. "I hope I didn't interrupt anything."

"We're fine," I said sourly. I turned to Ford. "Thanks for the backup, but I think we got it from here."

"Do you want a ride back to the diner for your car?"

"Lily can take me." I looked at my friend. She hiccupped and waved at Ford, a silly smile plastered on her cute-as-a-button face. "Or I can drive her. I'll just get my car in the morning."

He shrugged. "Good idea. I'd hate to have to run in your friend for drunk driving."

Damn it. Why did he have to sound so mad at me all the time?

Oh, maybe because you rocked his world with a sloppy drunken kiss. Still, I wouldn't take the blame for him being alone. One, I didn't know. And two, I didn't magically make it happen. Or did I? I'd been so infatuated with Ford... No, I wouldn't even think that. My magic was unpredictable, but I would have known if I'd tried to cast a soul-joining spell on him. Even so, I wasn't a shifter. I shouldn't be smelling any kind of mating scent.

I placed Tizzy on my shoulder and looked at my

tipsy friend. "Come on, Lily." To Ford, I said, "Thanks for the information about the case. I do appreciate it." He stared at me as if waiting for something more, so I added, "We'll talk about the other stuff later. I promise."

"Fine," Ford said. "Get home safe."

I took Lily's keys from her and dragged my two pals to Lily's truck. I didn't want to think about Officer Hottie or the bombshell he'd dropped on me. I wanted to think about Danny and the case. Frank's threat made me think that maybe the douche-y beaver knew something he hadn't reported to the police.

I heard Ford's truck back down the road. I didn't look back. I missed him already, and that wasn't the kind of thing that was going to help in my investigation.

"I think it's time we talked to a few of Danny's friends."

"What a sweet, sweet beaver," Tizzy drunkenly crooned.

"Stop saying beaver," I said.

"Beaver, beaver, beaver," she sang.

"Oh, dear Goddess."

Lily put her hand on my arm. "Maybe you should wait until tomorrow." She gestured to the partying shifters. "At least until people are sober."

A squeaky hiccup made me nod. I'd never get any

real answers with a drunk familiar on my hands. "Fine. Tomorrow."

Lily handed me the keys. "You drive."

"I have beaver fever," Tiz sang. "Baby, baby, baby, oh."

"No more partying for you."

"Spoilsport."

"That's me." I stroked Tiz's head fondly. "Special Agent Spoilsport." I had a feeling she wasn't the only one who thought so.

CHAPTER 7

I HAD several hours to kill before my meeting with the coalition, so I tracked down the addresses to a few of the witnesses, including one Carla Wells, a raccoon shifter, and Danny's on-again-off-again girl-friend. Lily dropped me at Lolo's so I could get my car. I drove to Fantasy Lane in a sketchy part of town, which, given the current state of Paradise Falls, meant it was really bad. Carla's place was a small one-bedroom trailer on cinder blocks. A rusty orange hatchback was parked out front near an overflowing trash barrel.

I knocked on the door. A thin young woman, with large brown eyes and a cigarette between her index and middle finger, opened the door and raised her brow at me. "If you are selling, I'm not buying, honey. This is Paradise, and I've got all I need." Her tone was wary, not sarcastic.

"I'm Special Agent Hazel Kinsey." I flashed my badge. "I'm investigating Daniel Mason's death. I believe you knew the victim."

Her hard edge softened. "Come in."

We sat at a small round kitchen table. The vinyl chairs were yellow, a bit worn, but clean. Her easy invite told me she wanted the investigation, so I didn't mess around. "According to the police report, you were the last person to see Danny alive," I said.

"Probably."

Carla blew smoke in my face. I waved it away. "Did he say anything that might give you the impression he was in danger?"

"Danny and me," Carla said. "We didn't talk much about personal things. Mostly, he just liked to talk about cars." She dabbed the glowing cigarette butt into an overflowing ashtray and blew out the last puff. "He really liked cars. He'd been working on an old Chevelle. He called her Sweet Beast. It really got him going, talking about that car." She snorted a laugh. "He used to razz me hard about my piece-of-crap rust bucket out there." Her eyes grew wistful. "I really miss him."

"You really cared for Danny."

"Of course, I did," she said. "He was my mate."

Had Lily known? I'd just found out about the shifter-mate thing the night before, so I wasn't sure if this was something they would have told anyone else. "Did his family know?"

Carla shook her head. "I told my mother, who told me it was impossible. A cougar shifter can't mate with a raccoon shifter. She made me promise to never speak of it again." Her hands were shaking now. "He smelled like lemon sorbet," she said. "He said when he was around me, the world smelled like lilacs on a hot summer day."

She looked me dead in the eyes. "I don't care what they say, Danny's death wasn't related to drugs. He'd quit doing them a couple of months before he died. He said as long as he had me, he didn't need to get high." She wiped her nose on the back of her hand, then reached back and searched the small kitchen counter behind her and grabbed a napkin. She dabbed her eyes and nose. "If you are serious about finding out what happened to him, I want to help."

Her pain turned her from witness to another victim in my estimation, and suddenly, I added her name to the list of people in my life who needed justice. The not-doing-drugs was a twist, though, because the autopsy report said he'd had trace amounts in his system. If he'd gone two months, the amount should have been zero.

"Are you sure he was off drugs?"

Carla nodded. "We both were." She absently

placed her hand on her stomach. "I'd even quit smoking."

Danny had died six months ago, but Carla's light touch on her flat tummy had me wondering. "Were you pregnant?"

She let her hand drop to her side, then grabbed another cigarette from an open pack on the table. She tapped the filter end on the surface. "We were making plans," she said. "He was taking care of me. Or at least trying to. He'd even bought me this place for us, so we could start our lives together." She raised her gaze from the cigarette to me, her eyes haunted with what could have been. "I'm not pregnant now."

The way she said it made me feel ill. I could tell she was done speaking on this topic, so I moved on to my next question. "Did Danny have any enemies? Anyone he was fighting with prior to his...death?"

"Oh, sure." She smiled, but it didn't reach her eyes. "Danny fought with all sorts. He got rousted by the police at least once a month whether he was doing anything wrong or not. And Clayton Driver, the owner of Junkyard Dog, said Danny owed him money for parts. He tried to collect from me after, but like I told the fool, you can't squeeze blood from a rock."

"How much did he owe Clayton?"

"Five grand." She sheeshed. "It might as well

have been five million. Even though he was trying, Danny never had that kind of money."

"Do you think Clayton would have killed Danny over the debt?"

"Clayton wants his money. You can't collect from the dead." She shook her head. "Besides, Clayton would have had him work off his debt before doing anything violent."

"Anyone else, Carla?"

"Not that I can think of." She bit her lower lip. "I heard Danny say something about the Arete once." She clenched her fist, crushing the unlit cigarette. "He sounded real scared."

"Who?"

She took another cigarette from her half-smoked pack. "I don't know. When I asked him, he clammed up about it. He made me swear to never speak of it again." She waved her lighter. "But I told the cops after his death, and here I'm telling you." She shook her head. "I never was good at doing what I was told."

There had been nothing in the file about Clayton Driver or any person or group called the Arete. Why would Mitchell, the lead detective on the case, leave that part of the interview out of his reports?

"The Arete—"

Carla cut me off. "I have to go, Agent Kinsey. I

clerk at Gabe's Green Grocery, and my boss said he'd fired me if I was late again."

I nodded. Jobs were scarce, especially in a small town. "If you think of anything else," I handed her my card, "you'll call me?"

"Sure," she said, taking the card and tucking it into her purse. "I..." She chewed her lower lip for a moment then turned her gaze to mine. "I'm glad someone's looking into what happened to Danny. There's more of us that care than don't." She shrugged. "He didn't deserve what happened to him."

"No one does," I agreed. Though if I got ahold of the bastard who killed him, I might make an exception.

It was unseasonably cool for late June, so I'd worn a jacket in the morning, but by the afternoon, it had warmed up quite a bit. I took it off when I parked just outside Junkyard Dog. A note fell out of the pocket. "Thank you. L." I smiled. She used to leave me notes in my pockets when we were kids. Stone Age text messages.

Really though, I should have been the one thanking *her*. Lily had saved my bacon more times than I could count when we were girls.

I'd called Lily after I'd left Carla's. I didn't tell her about the mating bond between her brother and the raccoon shifter, nor did I tell her about the implied pregnancy. She was already mourning enough loss; she didn't need more on her plate. My friend told me she knew who Clayton Driver was, but she hadn't known Danny owed him money. The junkyard owner was a werecougar like Lily and Danny, and he had been a business friend of her father's. She'd really wanted to come with me to talk to the man, but I convinced her to stay home and take care of Tiz. The squirrel was struggling to recover from a whopping hangover. She hadn't even remembered getting hit in the face by a beaver's tail.

Junkyard Dog, ironic name since Driver was a cat shifter, was down a rough gravel road on the Merry County line. Half the property was on Lister, the county that bordered ours, which would have made it a nightmare for law enforcement, considering jurisdiction would always be in question. Which made it a perfect location for criminal activity.

The strong scent of dust and rust made my skin itch. Even in broad daylight, the place, with all the vehicle skeletons stacked up like bodies after a battle, gave me the creeps. There a dilapidated trailer with a sign with the word "management" on the front. Just past that was a large building, about half the size of a basketball court. It had two large sliding doors, and one side was partially open.

The office was closed and the door locked. I yelled, "Hello. Is anyone here?" When I didn't get an answer, I strolled to the big metal building. "Hello," I said again.

I could see a car up off the ground on a lift. A series of hooks and chains hung from the ceiling. Before I could see more, a tall man with short red hair appeared from the open door.

"What can I do for you, miss?" He wore dungarees and a stained blue t-shirt, and he held a large wrench in his right hand. "Are you looking for parts?"

Even without a shifter nose, I could smell a combination of gas, diesel, and oil. "Are you Clayton Driver?"

"That would be me." He nodded at me. "Who's asking?"

I held out my badge. "Special Agent Kinsey, FBI. I have some questions I'd like to ask you."

"Do I need a lawyer?" He laughed. His green eyes crinkled at the corners.

"Not yet," I said. "I just have a few questions about Daniel Mason."

"Why?" He raised his left brow. "He's dead. Some drug deal gone bad, or so I've heard."

"That's what people are saying," I replied blandly. I didn't like this guy one bit.

He frowned. "Then I don't know how I can help you, Agent Kinsey."

"I heard Danny owed you money."

"It's Danny, now, huh? Is this investigation of yours personal somehow, Special Agent?"

"Answer the question."

He shrugged, wiped off his wrench with a rag, and set it down. "A lot of people owe me money."

I was getting tired of this dance. "Did you kill Danny Mason because he owed you money?"

Driver squinted at me, his hand raising to shield his eyes from the sun. "Do I know you?" He walked toward me, his long stride closing the distance between us fast.

I put my hand on my holster but didn't draw my weapon.

"You're the witch. The one the Mason girl was always running around with."

"You didn't answer my question." I patted the Glock. "Did you kill Danny?"

Driver shook his head. "Of course not, girl. I tried to look out for that kid." He glared at me. "I'm not a good man, but I don't murder my own kind." He took the few steps up to his office trailer and unlocked the door. "Can I make an observation, Agent Kinsey?"

"If it will shed some light on Danny's death, then go right ahead."

"You're out of your depth on this."

"Thanks for the advice." Before he could step inside, I asked, "What can you tell me about Arete?"

Driver stopped cold, his fingers clenching on the door handle. He hopped down the three steps to the ground, dust kicking up around his heels. He closed the distance between us fast enough to startle me. "What do you know about the Arete?"

The Arete? So it was a group. "Only the name."

Relief eased the tension in his eyes. "If you were smart, you'd keep it that way." He walked back up the steps. "Good day, Ms. Kinsey." He stepped inside the trailer and closed the door behind him.

CHAPTER 8

DRIVER HADN'T KICKED me off his property, so I took it as permission to look around. The rows of cars went back farther than I'd first thought, and the junkyard reminded me of the Tardis in *Doctor Who*, smaller looking on the outside and larger on the inside. I didn't know what I thought I would find, but it couldn't hurt to look.

My magic wasn't all that strong, and with Danny gone for four months, I didn't know if it would do me any good, but I tried my hand at a location spell.

"What I seek is what I find.

Danny Mason on my mind.

Hot or cold, let me see.

Trace Danny, so mote it be."

My hands began to glow a bright blue, which meant I was cold. I held them out in front of me, surprised I'd managed the magic in the first place without something exploding, and walked down one of the lanes. Blue still.

When I got to the last car, I cut around the back stack of cars and began walking up the next lane. The blue didn't change. It remained the same for every row I passed through.

Useless, I thought, and started back to my car, but when I crossed the open lot, my hands began to burn.

I looked down at them. Bright orange.

I was hot now. I resisted the urge to celebrate the minor victory. Instead, I followed my magic flames directly to the large barn behind the office. The interior was dark, and it took a moment for my eyes to adjust. The car up on the hydraulic lift was a beat up old Chevy muscle car. Tires, hubcaps, side panels, bumpers, and a variety of grills filled the large space. The walls featured shelves of carburetors, hoses, distributors, and other small car pieces. There were tool boxes, an acetylene torch setup with a mask, and lots of other equipment I couldn't name. Basically, what I'd expect to see in a junkyard garage.

An air compressor kicked in, and I stumbled in surprise.

My flaming hands were turning red now. Superhot. Danny had been here. A lot. I walked around the backside of the Chevy. It had a squared-off end, and the model was a Chevelle. Could it be Danny's

"Sweet Beast"? The one his girlfriend Carla had mentioned? The doors were off, but it was too high up for me to easily get inside. I would have tried levitating, but the last time I cast that particular spell, I'd ended up on the ceiling of my high school gym, and it had taken two hours to chant myself down. Talk about humiliating.

When Clayton Driver didn't show up to boot me out, I decided to press my luck. The panel for the lift had two buttons. Up and down. Efficient.

I pushed the down button. The level of screeching as the car lowered was jarring.

"Crap!" I hit the up button. The car reversed but the noise the lift made got even louder. "Noooo," I whined quietly.

I hit the down button again. Where the hell was the off switch? I cowered behind a trash barrel near the welder as I waited to be caught. No one came through the doors. The noise stopped when the car reached the ground.

After a few seconds of silence, I breathed a sigh of relief and came out of hiding. The interior wasn't nearly as rough as the exterior. It had a manual transmission. An eight ball, fairly cliché for a muscle car, had been drilled and set as the shifter knob. The seats were worn leather, old and a little stretched, but not cracked or torn. A shiny object hanging from the rearview mirror caught my eye.

It was a flower charm and a glass prism hanging from a silver chain. Not just any flower. It was a lily, and it was the same charm Lily used to wear around her neck when we were teenagers. This had to be Danny's fixer-upper. I opened the glove box. Fast food napkins, ibuprofen, motion sickness medicine, and lip balm littered the small cubby.

Shifters could get hurt, Danny and Boyd were proof they weren't indestructible, but I'd never in my life known a shifter to get a headache, let alone motion sickness. His girlfriend was a wereraccoon, so who else had Danny been spending time with? A human or a witch? And if he wasn't, what could cause a shifter to need these medications?

I put my hand on the dash and felt a rough patch. A closer look revealed a barely scratched-in capital H, just like the one I'd seen on Boyd's dresser. Who was this mysterious H? I snapped a quick picture with my phone then reached up to check the visor.

At that moment, an arm stretched around me, and a ginormous hand clamped over my mouth.

I screamed, but it sounded more like a muffled grunt. My arms were held tight to my sides, but I swung my fingers backed reflexively. My defensive magic, a little wild with my panic, zapped my assailant, releasing the aroma of roasted cinnamon in the air.

"Ouch, crap." Ford Baylor's low baritone made

my heart skitter. "Shhh," he added. "Someone is coming."

I nodded, and Ford lifted his hand from my face.

"What the hell, Ford?" I whispered harshly.

He glared at me and put his finger to his lips then pointed to the door. "Move," he mouthed.

I slid out of the car, Ford's large body moving after me with a lot more grace than I thought possible with his frame. He directed me to where some four-foot by eight-foot sheets of plywood rested against the back wall. We crawled behind just as the door to the building opened wide.

Maniacally, I had to suppress the urge to giggle as his breath ghosted my neck from behind. Goddess, when it came to this guy, I was in seriously deep bear doo-doo.

"Why is this car down?" I heard Clayton Driver say. "I swear to Goddess, Frank. I told you to leave the Chevelle alone."

"It was up when I last saw it," Frank said. I recognized his voice. It was definitely the beaver shifter Frank who'd tried to beat Tiz with his tail the night before.

The smell of snickerdoodles made it hard to concentrate on the words. I turned to look at Ford, my lips thin with irritation. He stared back at me, and my stomach quivered. His lip curled into a sexy-ass snarl as his light blue eyes undressed me...or at least that's the way I saw it.

I was going to tell him to kiss off, but instead, my throat stopped working at the same time as my good sense. I leaned my face to his, our lips centimeters from touching, and he...

Sharply diverted his head away, and my lips brushed his stubbled jaw.

What. The. Hell? I mean, what the hell was I thinking? We were hiding from potential bad guys, and I was trying to live out my school girl fantasy with the popular quarterback under a piece of dusty plywood.

At that point, I'd missed anything else said by Driver and Frank, because it was hard to hear over the berating my brain gave my libido.

The sliding door to the building closed, and Ford crawled out first. He stood up, his fingers flexing and clenching as he rapidly paced in front of me.

"What?" I said, keeping my voice down. "I'm sorry."

"Can you poof us out of here?"

I raised a brow. "Poof?"

"You know, use your witch powers to transport us somewhere else," he whispered.

"If by somewhere else you mean the top of Mount Everest, or worse, the middle of the Atlantic

Ocean, then sure, I could poof us out of here," I whispered back.

He stopped in his tracks and turned his gaze on me. "Fine." He looked around. "There's an opening in the siding over there." He pointed to the north wall. "Let's go."

"Why are you here at the junkyard?" I asked. "Are you following me?"

"You accused us of dropping the ball on Danny's murder. And now with Boyd Decker's death, I agree with you. It wasn't my case, but I knew Mitchell wasn't doing everything he could." Surprisingly, he grabbed my hand, and the intensity in his eyes made my knees weak. "I want to help you, but I also want…" He didn't finish.

"What else do you want?"

His gaze was stark as he pinned me with it. "I want to keep you safe, you daft woman." He shook his head. "Why did you come back here, Haze?"

"You asked me that already, and I told you. I came to bring Danny's killer to justice."

"Is that all?" His mouth pursed as he waited for my answer.

What could I tell him? That I never stopped thinking about him? That every man I met couldn't hold a candle to the intensity of my feelings for him?

Yes, I could have told him all of that, but I didn't. I was not ready for that conversation, and this situation, when Driver might come back at any moment, was not the right place or time for it.

Instead, I said, "We should skedaddle while the skedaddling is good."

"Is that your expert opinion or are you just avoiding the bear in the room?"

"Yes," I told him, "to both questions. Driver could come back at any minute."

We heard a truck engine roar to life. Ford went to the front door and peered around the corner. I followed him. He turned to me. "They've left," he said. "Both of them. We're alone." Then he grabbed me gently but firmly by the arms and lifted me up until my toes barely touched the ground and...he kissed me. Just a quick brush. Nothing more.

When he set me back down, I couldn't feel my feet, and I think my brain had short-circuited as well. I froze in place because all I knew was if I tried to move, I'd end up jumping up on Mt. Baylor and scaling him until the air was too thin to breathe.

He lowered his face to mine, his fingers curling under my chin, and said in the sexiest motherlovin', panty-melting, lust-inducing way, "Don't kid yourself, woman. Danny isn't the only reason you came back."

I would have protested, but my tongue refused to do anything but wag.

"For years, I've been a man half alive...until I saw

you yesterday, Haze. I can't go back to that. I can't go back to being someone who doesn't care whether a murderer is caught or not." Just as suddenly, he let me go. "My truck is parked about a mile down the road. Meet me at my place. I live at 216 Harmony Street. Do you need directions?"

I found my voice, finally. "I have GPS on my phone," I rasped.

The corner of his mouth tugged up. "We'll meet up in an hour."

"You want me to come to your house?"

"The chief has given us all direct orders to appear cooperative without cooperating. I want to help you, Haze, but not at the expense of my job."

"Can you make it three hours?" I had the meeting with Adele Adams and the coalition, and after that, I wanted to touch base with Lily.

"Fine." He nodded. "See you in three."

He nodded once then ducked down to slide out the side of the building.

When he was out of sight, I let out a stuttering breath and a quiet sob. Goddess, that man made every part of me want to touch every part of *him*. It was unnatural.

When the cinnamon scent faded, I left to get my car and headed back into town.

CHAPTER 9

THE WITCH-SHIFTER COALITION office was down on Heavenly next to the DMV. I spent the entire drive settling down my protesting libido and trying to get the feeling back in my lips. Damn, that Ford Baylor had really done a number on me. Again. If it weren't for Lily, I might have packed up my squirrel and got the hell out of Paradise Falls. I didn't have time for romantic complications. Especially from a tall, grumpy, and furry werebear.

Why did I let him kiss me? Even worse, I'd tried to kiss him first, and he'd cheeked me. It wasn't the first time I'd been kissed, and it hadn't even been the most passionate. Even so, it had rocked the very foundation of my world.

The alarm on my phone beeped. Shoot. I was late for my appointment. I cracked the windows of the car to vent the afternoon heat and went inside.

The coalition was housed in a historical brick two-story building with lead glass windows and large wooden double doors. I'd been there many times as a child, since my mother had been one of the members. It always felt creepy inside of their meeting room. I used to imagine the coalition would sacrifice animals and virgins alike.

Adele Adams—a tall, leggy blonde witch with big blue eyes that made her look doll-like—greeted me at the front desk. She wore a tightly fitted A-line dress with a deep vee in the front that showed off her buoyant breasts. She'd been on the board with my mother, and I didn't like her any better now than I did then, but I was determined to present polite professionalism.

"You're late, Agent Kinsey. I expected you to be here by noon." She tapped her watch. "I agreed, as a favor to Clementine, to meet with you. At the very least, you could be on time."

The way she'd said "Clementine" made me think she was trying a little too hard to prove she had a personal relationship with the Grand Inquisitor. From what I could gather through the witchvine, Adele was nearly one hundred and fifty years old and took great pride in her youthful appearance, which meant her magic probably packed a punch.

"Hi, Ms. Adams." I tried to look appropriately

contrite. "I'm sorry I'm late. Will any other members of the coalition be joining us?"

Her blue eyes darkened, and her expression grew suddenly intense. She lowered her gaze to mine and held my stare. "All of them."

"Great. I'm ready to start when you are."

She frowned as if disappointed. "Follow me." With a flick of her hand toward a door behind the desk, she turned on her four-inch heels and headed in that direction.

The backroom, which, as I said, creeped me out, reminded me of the temple rooms of the Freemasons or the Illuminati. Six ornately carved high-back chairs lined a stage-like area. Four people, two women and two men, sat in the four chairs on the right. The two on the left were empty. I recognized the man in the third chair, Dirk Nichols, the friendly neighborhood chief of police.

Behind the chairs was a red curtain. With dramatic flair, a man with dark hair stepped out of the shadows to reveal himself.

My stomach instantly felt leaden. "Dad?"

"Hazel, sweetheart." The handsome warlock, his green eyes flashing, took the second chair. His tailored suit fit him impeccably, but I knew his affability, much like his expensive clothes, was all window dressing.

I grimaced. "When and how did you get out of

jail?" I couldn't see Clementine Battles giving him early parole. Not even for good behavior.

"Seven months ago," he said. "I tried to contact you."

"I didn't get the memo." Outwardly, I affected indifference. Inside, anger clawed at me, a hungry dragon desperate to escape, but this wasn't the time or the place to have a showdown with Kent Kinsey. I took in the other four players in the room. If I focused on my purpose, Danny's murder, I thought I stood a chance of getting out of here without going into a patricidal rage.

"Hello," I said. "I'm here with permission from the Grand Inquisitor to investigate the suspicious death of Daniel Mason." I pulled out the white card, though no one seemed interested.

"Yes, yes," Adele said. "We are all aware that you are here with Clementine's blessing. Get on with your questions."

I pulled my smartphone out of my purse and slid out the stylus. "My notes," I explained when my action drew curious stares. "I have an app…"

Almost as a group, they blinked.

I shook my head. "Never mind. So, the coalition is made up of one witch, Adele Adams, two warlocks, the chief and Kent Kinsey." My mouth tasted bitter as I said his name. "And the three of you are?"

A woman, curvy with a bounty of strawberry-blonde hair, said, "Mary Lowe, matriarch for the *felidae*." I recognized the term and led with the assumption that she was the big momma to large cat shifters, like Lily and Clayton Driver.

"Robert Townsend." I recognized him as the small animal shifter from the station. "Nice to see you again, Agent Kinsey." He greeted me with congeniality. "You already know I'm the leader of the *paullulum mammalia*. I, myself, am *raton*."

"And that is?" I hoped it wasn't what I thought it was because I had a real problem with rats.

His brow furrowed, then he smiled again. "It's just a fancy name for a raccoon therianthrope," he said.

"Bob represents the interests of badgers, chipmunks, and raccoons in town," Mary said.

"The non-predators," Chief Nichols said.

My father chuckled, and with a great charm that I'd known and loved as a child, he said, "They're half human, Dirk. That means they are all predators. No matter the size."

I rolled my eyes and refused to make eye contact. I agreed completely, but I wasn't ready to acknowledge him. "And you are," I said to a large man, at least six-foot-six with dark hair and gray eyes.

He stepped toward me with his hand out. "I'm

Bryant Baylor, *Arcturus,* alpha for the bear shifters in Paradise Falls."

Gulping, I shook his hand. His palm practically swallowed my hand to the wrist. This was Ford's dad. "Nice to meet you, sir." Goddess help me. What were the chances that my father and Ford's father were both in the coalition? It seemed astronomically impossible, but here they were.

"We should get down to business," Adele said. "I have other engagements today."

"Of course, Ms. Adams," I said. Some of the hard-wood planks in the floor squeaked as I walked across the room. In front of the high-back chairs was a rectangular desk. The top reached my hips. I set my phone down and looked at Adele. "If there are a couple of small chairs, we can do the interviews right here."

She nodded. Mary and my father retrieved two metal folding chairs. The desk was hand carved. The essence of the wood felt old under my fingertips. I placed my palms on the surface, and the wood began to glow with a white current. I lift my hands. The current died. "What is this thing made of?"

"It's a combination of birch elm, elder wood and, interestingly, hazel wood," my father said, "for which you were named."

I glared at him. This wasn't a happy family reunion, and I wished like hell he'd quit acting like he hadn't been in jail for almost two decades for using black magic to dispatch my mother. He shrugged and gave me a half-smile. I resisted the urge to give him the full finger.

There was an old leather-bound book in the center of the desk that was at least twelve inches wide by eighteen inches long and as thick as Dick Knuckles' head, with an unusual fractal symbol tooled into the cover. Next to it was an all-white athame, a traditional double-sided blade used by witches and warlocks. It was the kind of weapon that had created the sacrificial nightmares of my youth, but I'd never seen one quite like this. I picked it up. It was cold to the touch and amazingly light. Symbols had been carved into the blade and handle, but I'd never been much good with rune work or the Theban alphabet, so I couldn't tell what they meant.

The wood in the desk was alive with energy. It made me wonder why the blade felt dead.

I slid my finger over the tip. It was dull. "Huh."

Someone took the ornamental knife from me with one quick snatch. I looked up and blinked as Adele Adams put it back on the desk near the book.

"Please don't handle the artifacts in this room," Adele said with a tight-lipped smile. "We keep various historical pieces that originate from both sides of our community in here. They are for looking, not touching."

I didn't really believe the coalition was hiding things from me, but this seemed like a group with secrets, so I quietly spelled.

"What is it that I must not see?

Second sight, so mote it be."

The entire room began to glow, with the exceptions of Mary Lowe and the red curtain.

Hmm. I hadn't been thinking of anything specific when I murmured the spell, so the only thing this told me for certain was that the cat shifter was the only one with nothing to hide. Interesting. I casually scanned the room until my gaze landed on Adele, her eyes wide.

"What did you do?"

CHAPTER 10

WELL, damn. Usually, I was the only one who could see the result of the location spell. I reminded myself this witch was old and raised my hands. "Whoops. Sorry."

"What happened?" Nichols asked.

Adele ignored him. "How did you do that?"

I ignored the chief as well. "It's a simple reveal spell." And much like her ta-tas, there was much to expose here at the coalition.

She narrowed her gaze at me. The glow in the room disappeared. Adele's voice took on an ominous quality, and I could feel the power she shoved into her words. "There is nothing simple about a reveal spell, child."

As far as intimidation went, Adele Adams was a master. She ranked right up there with the Grand Inquisitor for the Scary Bitch of the Week award.

"Uhm." Time for a change in subject. "Are you all familiar with Danny Mason's death?"

The shifters nodded, but the witch and the warlocks were still looking at me like I'd sprouted horns and grown a third ear.

"Good." I ignored the magic half of the coalition and pulled up my notes on Danny. "Are you aware of the extent of the damage done to his body before he was killed?"

Bryant Baylor cleared his throat. "I know from the chief there was an extreme number of broken bones in his body."

"Yes." I nodded. "All of them. With the last bone, a rib, stabbing into his heart."

Mary Lowe gasped. "I didn't know all that. I thought he was mugged for drugs or something like that. How in the world did he suffer that many injuries?"

"That's a great question, Ms. Lowe. One that I'm trying to find the answers for." I scanned the others in the room. "You all are the leaders in this community. There is hardly anything that happens that you wouldn't know about."

"Are you accusing us of something, Mizz Kinsey?" Chief Nichols asked. His sandy-blond hair rose with his ire as if pulled upward by a static charge.

"Not yet," I said. "But I'm beginning to think

maybe I should. And I'd like Detective Dennis Mitchell to be made available to me too." I was tired of playing nice. "This case was handled with an ineptitude I've never seen in all my years in law enforcement. He is either the worst police officer ever, or he is hiding something. Maybe on your orders."

Chief Nichols jumped to his feet. "You uppity little witch." His hands flung out toward me as his lips moved quickly. The hair on my arms stood on end as he gathered magic for the spell.

I pulled my handgun from its holster and patted it against my thigh. He might be better at witchcraft, but I was betting I could blow a hole in him faster than he could hit me with whatever he was working on. "Bring it," I said.

Nichols flew back through the curtains with a surprised howl of anger and shock.

I shook my head. "I didn't do that."

"I did," my father snarled. Nichols staggered back into the room, his hands bathed in a red glow. I aimed my weapon, but my father stepped between us, his back to me as he faced the chief. "Enough!"

Dirk staggered back as if he'd been slapped by the word.

"There's no call for anyone to be uncivil," Adele chimed in. She gave Nichols a meaningful look. Instantly, he backed down. "Just what information do you want from us, Agent Kinsey?"

I put my weapon away as a show of good faith but kept my hand near the holster. "Boyd Decker was killed yesterday in his home. His death is too much like Danny's to be a coincidence. And from what I saw, there is not a human or shifter in this world that could have misshaped the wereraccoon into the blob he'd become. It's physically impossible."

"I didn't detect any magic on Danny," my dad said.

"You were there?" My stomach sank.

"The chief asked me to verify his finding of no magic." His expression soured. "It wasn't witchcraft that killed Daniel Mason."

"And Boyd Decker wasn't touched by our magic, either," Nichols added. "We're not trying to cover up any crimes here, Kinsey. Regardless of what fantasies you've cooked up in your head."

I couldn't argue because I hadn't felt any magical residue either, but whatever had disfigured and tortured Danny and Boyd wasn't purely physical. There was a sophistication to their executions that would require more finesse than brute force.

Adele seemed unperturbed by the entire exchange. "Those are not questions. I thought you wanted to interview us, Hazel, but this feels more like an indictment."

"Fine," I said. "Who's practicing dark magic in Paradise Falls?" Poignantly, I looked at my father.

He sighed. "I paid for my crimes, Hazel. I'm a witch-law-abiding warlock these days."

Too bad he hadn't been so abiding when he'd killed my mother using forbidden magic. I turned to Adele. "You are potent with magic, Ms. Adams."

"Yes," she agreed.

"And you didn't feel anything unusual had caused these deaths."

"You still haven't asked a question."

"Do you know who killed Danny Mason and Boyd Decker?"

"No," she said simply and without elaboration.

I looked around the room. The other five members were shaking their heads. I saw something in Bryant Baylor's eyes that I recognized right away. A simmering fury.

"I find that hard to believe. It takes something seriously dark to turn a man's insides into kindling sticks."

"Are you sure about that?" Kent asked. "If magic is the culprit, and it is black by nature, the Grand Inquisitor and her minions would have been all over this town looking to punish the culprit."

"You would know," I countered.

His mouth turned down at the corner. Well, boo-freaking-hoo. "I don't possess any black magic, Hazel. I'll admit that the magic I used was corrupt, but there was nothing inherently evil about it."

"Tell that to Mom."

He looked as if I'd slapped him across the face, but he didn't deny it.

"You're not a child anymore, Hazel," Adele said. "You are old enough to understand that your mother—"

Kent cut her off. "Enough, Adele. Hazel can believe what she wants to believe. It's of no consequence."

I narrowed my gaze. What was my dad keeping from me? Now wasn't the time for personal revelations. I needed answers about Danny's murder. "Have any of you heard of the Arete?"

Mary and Chief Nichols blanched. Baylor glowered. Adele, my dad, and Robert Townsend had blank, unreadable expressions.

"Where did you hear that name?" Baylor growled.

"Why does everyone get so antsy and nervous whenever I bring the name up?"

Adele clucked her tongue against her teeth. "Arete isn't a group or a person, Agent Kinsey. It's a state of being. A striving for excellence in all things. To be arete is to be morally, mentally, and physically virtuous."

"Why would Danny be scared when talking about the Arete then?"

"I have no idea."

"Mizz Kinsey, you are barking up the wrong tree on this Danny Mason business. The boy was into stuff that would have gotten anyone killed, shifter, witch, or human. He was bad news."

"That is Special Agent Kinsey, to you, Dick. And I think the narrative around Danny Mason has been exaggerated. From what I've learned, he was trying to get his life together."

"And who did you hear this from?" the chief asked.

I glanced at Robert Townsend and remembered how private Carla had been about being Danny's mate. I wouldn't expose her confession, not in this room with these people. "I've been investigating," I told him. "It's what good cops do."

"For your information, there is a group of meth-amphetamine producers out of northern Missouri, who have been trafficking drugs up into Iowa. If you check with your FBI, I'm sure they can corroborate what I'm saying. These folks have been flying under the radar, and it's made it difficult to catch them in the act of moving product. I suspect there are several young people in our community who help and work for them," Chief Nichols said. "I've been trying to stop them for over two years. I long suspected Daniel Mason was part of that group." He looped his thumbs into his black belt. "It wouldn't surprise me if Boyd was a part of their organization as well. The young man was a known drug offender."

I jammed my fists against my hips. "Danny only had trace amounts of opiates in his system. That is not someone who is heavy into meth."

Nichols smirked. "I said trafficking, not using. I thought you were the *good cop*. Maybe you should pay attention."

Robert Townsend pounded his fist against the desk. "That's enough, Dirk." He strode to the chief. "I've known John and Joy Decker my entire life. They are my kin. I won't have you talking about their son that way. Not without real proof."

A hint of a smile tugged at Nichols' lips. "No offense, Bob. It's just a speculation."

"So you think some human meth heads had the skill to manipulate flesh and bone and to perpetrate these killings?"

Dirk Nichols' smug smile soured. "That's what I think."

"You really are a crap police officer, Dick."

"Just wait one damned minute," he protested.

Adele Adams held her hand up and silenced him. "Is there anything else you want to know, Agent Kinsey? As you can see, we are dealing with external forces in our town that we haven't quite figured out yet."

"You have to know magic is involved. There's no

way in hell a bunch of human yahoos twisted Danny and Boyd into pretzels. It might not be witchcraft, but it's definitely supernatural. Why haven't you insisted on a vigorous investigation?" I directed the question to Nichols and Adele.

"My man took the investigation as far as he could."

I snorted. Super businesslike. "You and I have both read Detective Mitchell's reports. There are enough holes in his inquiries to sink the *Titanic*. And I know from several witnesses that he left key details out of his notes."

"Are you questioning my integrity, Agent Kinsey?"

"Yes," I said with some exasperation. "I think I'm being pretty obvious about it."

The police chief turned red in the face, Adele Adams looked annoyed, but the rest of the group, including my dad and Bryant Baylor, seemed to be conveying quiet approval.

"I think we've given you enough of our time, Agent Kinsey." Adele started walking to the door. "You be sure and tell Clementine we cooperated."

"I certainly will," I mumbled. "I'll make sure the Grand Inquisitor gets an earful."

Once I stood outside the building on the concrete sidewalk, the June wind whipping through my hair, I breathed a giant sigh of relief. I'd learned three things: My dad was out of magic jail. There was tension between the shifters and the witches. And finally, the coalition was full of liar-liar-pants-on-fires.

Did Lily know my dad was back in town? If she did, why hadn't she told me? Ford had to know, but we weren't exactly friends so he might not understand the significance. Maybe Lily had been afraid that I wouldn't investigate her brother's death if she told me.

I pushed down the anxiety building in my chest and got back on the road to Lily's to find out if there was anything else she'd kept from me.

CHAPTER 11

I'D GONE STRAIGHT to Lily's house from the coalition meeting. My mind raced with all the possibilities, but there was only one that made any sense. Lily had kept this huge piece of information from me on purpose.

"I'm sorry I didn't tell you, Haze," she said, confirming what I'd suspected. She'd known my father was out of jail and back in this goddess-forsaken place and hadn't bothered to share this bombshell with me.

When I didn't immediately respond, she added, "When you left Paradise Falls, you hated him and hated this town. Your mother had...you know, and your father was in jail. You never looked back. I wanted to tell you when I called, but I was afraid if you knew Kent was out of jail, you wouldn't come home. I tried to tell you again when you got here, but then the whole Boyd tragedy happened."

I didn't know how to respond to Lily's confession. Hearing about my dad might've given me pause, but I still would've come home to help her, regardless of what it might cost me personally. Even so, I understood her reasoning.

I guess my silent contemplation must've freaked Lily out because she started talking a mile a minute. "You haven't called me or written to me since the day you left Paradise Falls, Hazel." Her voice quivered. "I'm desperate to find out what happened to my brother. He is...*was* the only family I had left. I wanted to tell you that Kent was back in town, I really did, but I couldn't take the chance that you'd change your mind about helping me find out who killed Danny. It's selfish, I know, but I raised Danny. He wasn't just my brother. In a way, he was like my child." Tears filled her eyes. "I'm sorry if I hurt you, but I'm not sorry that I got you here. Be mad at me if you must be, but please don't leave town. I need you."

Seeing her so upset shook me. I'd abandoned her, and I'd made her feel like the only way she could get my help was by not telling me the whole truth. Cripes, I'd been a real asshole.

"I'm not mad at you, Lily." I dropped my gaze to

the floor. "I wish you'd trusted me enough to tell me, but I get why you didn't. We don't really know each other anymore. Not the adult versions. In your head, I am still that eighteen-year-old teenager who left town as if she were being chased by a horde of hungry trolls and she was the last snack on Earth. And it's the same for me. In my head, I still think of you as my rowdy, ballsy BFF, my partner-in-crime, the person I could share everything with, but you're not. You've been through so much that I wasn't there for, and that's one hundred percent my fault." I put my hand on her thin-boned shoulder. "I want to fix all that, and working on your brother's case is a good place to start." I let my hand drop to my side. "I'm just still reeling about seeing my father, is all." It had been as if all the air had been sucked out of the room when he'd walked in, and I'd hated that he'd made me feel like a wounded kid all over again. I forced a smile for Lily. "We can talk more about it tonight."

"Will we?" I heard the apprehension in her voice.

"Yes, Lils." I made my reply gentle. "We will. Promise. But right now, I'm going to put Kent Kinsey on the backburner where he belongs and focus on your brother." Working the case was the only thing that would take my mind off my dad. I loved my dad, and I hated him.

"Did you learn anything new?"

"Yes, there is something," I told her, thinking about Ford's revelation about us the night before. Was I really so ignorant in the ways witches were different from shifters? "Are you mates with anyone?"

Her eyes widened. "Am I...huh?"

"Do you have a mate?" I asked again. "The whole mate-scent thing. Do you have that with someone?"

She shook her head. "I haven't found my mate. I honestly don't think he exists. At least not in Paradise Falls. What does this have to do with Danny?"

"Maybe nothing, but maybe something." I sat down on the sofa in her front room and allowed my shoulders to slump forward. "Can you tell me how it works?"

"How what works?"

"Mating. You know, for your...kind?"

Her face reflected genuine surprise and a little hurt. "You mean therianthropes. Shifters."

"Yes. Sorry. I didn't mean it to sound like I was lumping us into different groups. When we were growing up we never really discussed the things that made us different from each other, and I never realized just how ignorant I am when it comes to therianthropes." I pressed on. "Will you please explain to me how shifter mating stuff works?"

"When a mommy shifter and a daddy shifter love each other," she started.

I grimaced. "That's not what I mean. I'm not trying to get the low down on the birds and bees."

"Then you better tell me why you're asking," she said.

"Ford says we're mates. He says I smell like vanilla rum. For me, he smells like spicy desserts. What am I supposed to do with something like that?"

"Oh, Haze." She sat down next to me and took my hand. We intertwined fingers. "When did this happen?"

"Apparently, it happened during that bonfire right before our senior year. I was so drunk, I don't remember it, but according to him, I basically assaulted him with a kiss."

"Oh," Lily said. "I remember that night. We'd both had a snoot full, and you were obsessing about Ford, so I dared you to kiss him."

"Lily!"

"After that, my parents came and took us home. You never said anything about it, so I didn't think anything about it."

"Because I didn't remember," I told her. "But after that, I smelled baked cinnamon desserts every time I got around him. I had no idea why. I thought it was just a crazy crush." I shook my head. "Apparently, I smell like vanilla and rum to him." I looked at her. "Goddess on a bender. If I had known about shifter mate-scent stuff, I wouldn't have done it."

Lily looked confused. "Done what?"

My voice broke. "Cast a spell, or whatever I magic I'd conjured that night to make the stupid bear love me."

Lily chuckled softly. "It doesn't work like that. The mate-scent happens when two people who are fated come into physical contact with each other. It's why shifters date a lot." She gave my hand a squeeze. "Besides," she teased. "When you were a teenager, you couldn't cast your way out of a paper bag let alone cast your way into a relationship."

"That's true." I pulled a tissue from a box on her coffee table and dabbed at my eyes. "But what if I did it on accident?"

She shook her head and met my gaze. "If you and Ford caught each other's scent, then it was fated."

The idea that Ford and I were fated, that his attraction to me wasn't a choice, was a whole Pandora's box of issues that I wasn't ready to open. A thought occurred to me as I blew my nose. "Why do you have tissues? I thought shifters didn't get common illnesses like colds or flues. Or am I ignorant about that as well."

"Danny," she admitted.

"Oh, I'm so sorry. The grief..." I was a class A jerk. "I'm sorry for making this about me. I promise to keep my focus on Danny."

"It's okay. I'm happy for a little distraction, and, shifters can get sick, but you're right that it's not any of the common human ailments. We have a few viruses that can take us down for a few days, and seasonal allergies are fairly common," she added. "Even so, Danny had been getting sick a lot the last year of his life. I'd assumed it was the drugs. But he'd stopped informing me about his life as soon as he graduated from high school, so I don't know for sure."

"His friend Carla said he'd quit doing drugs eight months before he died. That he was cleaning up his life. But Nichols thinks he was part of some drug trafficking ring. Did you notice any differences in him the last couple of months before he died?"

She shook her head. "Other than him looking worn down, not really." She released my hand and rubbed her arms. "I'd stopped talking to him, Haze. A year earlier, he'd stolen all the money out of my purse and in an empty coffee can I'd hid behind a bunch of stuff in the pantry. It was over eight thousand dollar. It was all the money I'd managed to save since high school. My escape-Paradise-Falls fund."

She blinked tears back. "I turned my back on him because of something as stupid as money."

"What had he done with the money?"

"Probably bought drugs or used it to pay off some gambling debt."

Then I remembered Carla's trailer. "Oh, Lily. I think I know where the money went."

"Where?"

"He bought Carla Wells a small trailer out on Fantasy Lane. He was planning to move in with her."

She tucked her chin and frowned. "Why would he do that?"

I wasn't sure how she would feel about what Carla had told me about Danny, keeping it from her wasn't a choice. "Danny and Carla Wells were mates."

Lily's brow furrowed in confusion. "What do you mean?"

"According to Carla, they'd caught each other's scents."

"Predator animals don't mate with prey animals," she told me. "At least that's what I've always been told."

"Then how do you explain Ford and me?"

She shook her head. "I can't. Maybe because you're a witch. If you were human, it definitely wouldn't be possible. But Danny and Carla? I've never seen it happen."

"So prey doesn't mix with predator?"

"I've heard of one instance where a wereraccoon married a werebear, but they were never able to conceive a child. Real mated couples can breed. These two loved each other, but they never caught the scent that would bind their souls."

Soul-binding. Ford had said something to that effect. I took Lily's hand for the next information I was about to drop. "I think Carla had been pregnant."

Lily's voice raised an octave. "She had a baby? Danny's baby?"

I shook my head. "I don't think so. I think she had a miscarriage or maybe an abortion when he died. Either way, there's no baby. Not now."

Lily grabbed a tissue this time. "Then they *were* mated. Oh, Hazel. I feel like everything right side up is upside down. Why wouldn't Danny tell me this? Any of it? He wouldn't have had to steal from me. I would have helped him." She buried her face in her hands. "He was sober. He had a mate, a baby..." Her eyes brimmed with unhappiness. "I didn't know him at all."

I thought about my dad and mom, and how they had been so wrapped up in their busy lives that they hadn't paid a lot of attention to me. "You were a child yourself when you took on Danny to raise. You had to be his parent without any help from anyone.

Not even me. I saw you with him those months before I left for college. You were awesome with Danny. And sometimes, even kids raised in loving homes struggle. What happened to your brother wasn't your fault. You couldn't have done anything to prevent it. He was an adult who made his own choices."

She exhaled a noisy breath. "Thanks, Haze. I needed to hear that. Have you found out anything else?"

"There are clues, but nothing that points to anything concrete." I frowned. "Have you heard about something called the arete?"

"As in Queen Arete from *Homer's Odyssey*?"

We'd had to read the book in high school, but I'd bought the CliffsNotes version. "I don't remember her."

"She was described as the most honored woman on Earth." She sat up straight and asked with piqued interest, "Does this have something to do with the case?"

"I think so, but the honored woman part doesn't make any sense." I stood up. "Yet." I looked at the time. "I told Ford I'd stop by his house."

"Please don't be upset with me, Haze. You know, about your dad."

I felt the familiar pinch of pain. "I'm not upset

with you." She stood up, and I hugged her tight. "We're good."

I felt her relax as the tension she'd been holding eased. And I wished heartily that I could let my own go.

Fifteen minutes later, I turned onto Harmony. Ford's street. I parked on the curb in front of his pale green ranch-style house and put my head down on the steering wheel and closed my eyes. I'd never felt so exhausted. Seeing my dad, finding out he was out of jail, had taken an unforeseen emotional toll on me.

In my youth, many had described me as a "daddy's girl," and when he was taken by the witch police, I believed I never wanted to see him again. I still felt that way. My mother had never been an attentive parent. But my dad, well, he'd been different. Witches and warlocks who married sometimes went through a magical pairing ceremony that tied them together until death. My parents had been one of those pairings. They were obsessed with each other. I might not have felt my mother's love, but I'd seen it when she was with my dad.

When the tether between them had been cut, my mother perished into nothingness, and my father was arrested. It had all happened so quickly. I'd moved in with Lily and Danny to finish out the last month of high school, and the rest, as they say, was history. Or at least I thought so, but it turned out I'd left more than a broken youth behind.

The old familiar ache returned.

A sharp rap on the roof of my car startled me. I looked up to see Ford standing outside my door and staring at me. "You coming inside?"

"Yes," I said, willing my racing pulse to slow down. "I'm coming."

"I bet that's not the first time he's made a woman say that," Tizzy said.

I screamed. She screamed.

Ford yanked the door open and pulled me out of the car as if rescuing me from a pit of snakes. He shoved his head in the car, his body relaxing when he saw it was only Tizzy.

"Why did you scream?" Tiz asked. She clutched her chest dramatically. "I think you gave me a heart attack."

"I didn't know you were in the car! You scared the crap out of me."

"I thought something smelled bad." She waved her paw in front of her face, her tail swishing from side to side.

Ford chuckled.

I snapped my fingers at him and the squirrel.

"Not funny." I shifted my focus to my sneaky familiar. "How did you get in my car?"

"You left the window cracked about two inches. I'm pretty flexible. I do yoga, you know."

"You should have nama-stayed home with Lily." I sighed. "When did you get in my car?"

"Oh." She shrugged, her shoulders brushing her cheeks. "While you were in with the witch-were group. Lily told me about your dad. I thought you might need me, but then you were so upset, and I thought you might need someone to yell at, so I stayed out of sight."

She wasn't wrong about me needing someone to yell at, but it wasn't Lily. "Go back to Lily's," I demanded.

"Lily has been through a lot. She feels bad for keeping it from you. You can't blame her, though, for not telling you." Tiz's sincere defense of my oldest friend moved me.

"I don't blame her, okay? I promise you, we're good." I tipped her chin with my knuckle until her big brown eyes looked up at me. "So, go. Okay? I'll check in later, I promise."

I crossed my arms as I watched Tizzy climb up a nearby tree, jump onto the roof of a ranch house, take a flying leap off the far side, and disappear.

"She loves you," Ford said. His blunt observation rattled me.

"I know that." Some witches treated their familiars like tools, some as pets, but Tiz had always been more like family to me. A sister, of sorts. She kept me sane during an insane part of my life. I don't know that I'd have made it out of Paradise Falls if it weren't for her.

"Let's get inside." Ford gestured to his house. "I have the reports and witness statements laid out in the kitchen."

CHAPTER 12

FORD'S HOUSE WAS UNEXPECTED. It was a three-bedroom ranch house, with one bedroom converted to an office, and two bathrooms. A large kitchen with a stainless-steel convection oven, a gas range, a butcher block top center island, a double well stainless-steel sink, a peg wall full of high-end pots and pans, and granite counters. His side-by-side refrigerator was bigger than the clothes closet in my bedroom back home, and he had a large pantry. This was a kitchen for someone who loved cooking.

"Are you any good?" I asked when we moved to the center island. The surface was littered with photos, newspaper clippings, official reports and, oddly, two books that appeared well-read if the worn edges of their binding were any indication.

His brows raised. "Good at what?"

I warmed under his heated gaze.

"Chef-ing." I gestured to the room. "It's quite the kitchen." The dark brown curtains matched his hair color, and the pale blue walls complimented his eyes. Coincidence? "The choice of colors…"

"Tanya picked the colors."

Heat crept up my neck. "She did, did she?" My words sounded tight in my ears. It was taking every ounce of my control not to tear down the curtains and slash the walls with the knives in the butcher block caddy near the stovetop.

He noted my indignation and smiled. "Yep." He nodded. "As a favor."

"She sure likes to do you a lot of favors."

"You forfeited your right to be angry when you left me."

"Seriously? I didn't leave you. We never dated." His insistence that I should have somehow magically known we were mated tweaked my ire. "You act as if we were together. I'd never even so much as had a conversation with you, if you don't count the time in the lunch line when you asked me to hand you the catsup."

He shook his head as if to deny my words. "My life was good, Hazel. I got good grades. I had a nice girlfriend."

I choked a laugh. "Greta wasn't nice."

"She was to me," he said. "I had everything planned out for my future. I knew what I wanted to be when I got out of high school and who I wanted to be with. Then you came along one night, and on a drunken dare, you kissed me." His next words were almost hushed and reverent. "You changed me, Haze. When you did that, you changed everything."

I rolled my eyes. "I never knew just how transformative my lips were." I threw my hands up in the air. "If I'd have known that I could turn popular dicks into my love slaves, I might have kissed all the boys." I heard it as it left my mouth. I was being an asshole.

"You really know nothing about therianthropes, do you?"

"I know enough." But I really didn't. "My best friend is a freaking werecougar."

"Is she?" He glowered. "Is she your best friend? Before you returned to Paradise Falls, when was the last time you even talked to her? Do you even know what she's had to do to keep a roof over her and Danny's heads?"

His spicy scent became more pungently delicious with his anger. My lower bits throbbed to life, and my face flamed. The stupid bearman was giving me a bunch of crap about being a crappy person, and all I could think about was how much I wanted to conquer his peak with my valley.

I blew out a ragged breath and tried to focus. "That's not fair. I had to get away. I..." Left my friend behind. I sniffled. "My mom was dead. My dad responsible." *I didn't think I could ever have you.* I hadn't realized until that moment just how much Ford had affected me. "Why are you being so mean to me?"

He surprised me by wrapping his arms around me and pulling me into the warmth of his wide chest. "Because," he said, "I need you to understand that while witches can choose to pair with a magical binding, it's not a choice for shifters. We are mated whether you like it or not, without ceremony, for life."

The word "life" echoed in my head. "This is all so confusing."

"Two shifters are bonded by an overwhelming need to be together. There is always a unique scenting involved. For me, with you, it was vanilla and rum." He touched my hair and inhaled. "I can't even go into a bar because it makes me think of you."

"Is that why I smell cinnamon desserts every time I'm around you? I noticed it our senior year, but I just thought you'd changed colognes."

"I smell like cinnamon desserts?" His hands stroked my back.

"Cinnamon buns right now." Unwitch-like, I sniffed him. "It's making me really hungry." I hadn't eaten all day, but I wasn't just starved for food. I rose up on my tiptoes and kissed his neck.

Before we took this any further, there was something I had to know. "So you never had sex with Tanya Gellar."

"Nope."

"I don't need to know anything more," I said. I stroked his short beard, caressing the dark hair with my fingertips. I pressed my mouth against his, gentle and easy. I tugged his lower lip between my teeth and bit down—not hard enough to break the skin but hard enough to make him moan.

"Woman," he said, very caveman-like. His fingers wound up my neck and twined into my hair. My lips parted for him as he lifted me, and I wrapped my legs around his hips. I took his breath inside me as our mouths melded into a kiss that shot pleasure daggers to my groin.

I didn't even notice he'd carried me to his bedroom until he threw me down on the bed. "This is all a little sudden," I said, stripping my tank top over my head.

"I don't know," Ford said. "I think a couple of decades doesn't make for sudden."

He pulled his shirt off, his broad chest peppered with dark hair, and his cut-from-steel abs had grooves deep enough to scale.

"It should be illegal for you to wear a shirt." I stared at his pecs as they danced when he crawled up the bed to me. I let out an unsteady breath. "Like go-to-jail, do-not-pass-go kind of illegal."

"You have too many clothes on." He unbuttoned my pants and slid them down my thighs. "That's better."

He spread my legs, his thumbs tracing inner thigh. Weirdly, my witch magic crackled like electricity along my skin. That was new.

He drew his finger back as a spark licked the tip. "Is this going to be a problem?" he asked.

"Uhm…" Maybe. "Nope. I've got it under control." I willed my magic to stop cock-blocking me. Ford's hair raised on his arms and chest as more energy crackled. "I don't want to electrocute you. We should probably stop."

"Uh-uh." He unbuttoned his jeans. "I'll take my chances."

"Thank the Goddess." I did not want him to stop.

Ford's body stilled. "Don't, Haze."

"Why?"

"How bad do you want to have sex right now?"

My whole body vibrated with lust and desire. "Pretty freaking bad."

"Me too."

"Then what's the problem?" I rubbed myself against him. "I want you. You want me."

"Because of the mating drive."

I leaned back to gauge his expression. "What?"

He shook his head. "You really don't know much about shifters."

"I think we've established that already."

"The mating drive happens as a byproduct of the mating scent. If we take this further, I'm not sure I'll have the willpower not to take it all the way."

"All the way…"

"To the mating bite, which will seal our fate forever."

"You mean…" I got the gist, but I wanted him to spell it out.

"It means I'll never let you go, Hazel. If you push me, and we mate as mates, you'll have to give up your life outside our world. Or I'll have to leave my life to follow you."

"Would that be so bad?"

"Yes." He got up and put on his clothes. It made me want to shoot him. Unhappily, I followed his lead.

When we were back in the kitchen, I wrapped my arms as far around his waist as I could, and I held him tight. "I have never stopped thinking about you, Ford. I've never dated anyone because they weren't you. I threw myself into my work, believing that the job would be enough for me. I don't remember our kiss, and I'm sorry it changed you into something you didn't want to be, but for me, I hadn't needed some biological imperative to tell me that you were the boy I wanted to love. I had feelings for you long before you started smelling like cinnamon toast."

He tried to pull away, but I buried my face in his chest.

"We don't have to hash this out right now," I said quickly, "but I need you to stop being angry at me. Especially since I didn't know that you had this... reaction to me."

He stroked my hair, melting me. "You make mating sound like an allergy."

I chuckled. "I couldn't stand watching you with Greta. Don't you see?" I tilted my head back again to look at him. "I can't tell you how many times I wanted to cast a spell to make all her hair fall out." I didn't mention that the only reason I didn't cast the spell on Greta was because I sucked. The first and only time I'd practiced the spell, I'd aimed at my pee-my-pants dolly, but the magic went sideways, and poor Tizzy ended up bald for a month. Bald is not a good look for flying squirrels. "I never meant to hurt you, Ford."

Which meant, I really didn't know much about his or Lily's kind at all.

Ford kissed my forehead. "I'm not mad at you, Haze."

His blue eyes blinked down at me.

I smirked. "Vanilla and rum, huh?"

"You've really never even dated anyone?"

"You're the only person I've ever wanted to date."

"What about sex?"

I shook my head. "Not with someone else," I smirked. I might have been a thirty-eight-year-old virgin, but I wasn't asexual. "Masturbation can take the edge off."

He laughed. "You're not kidding."

"You?"

"Not with someone else," he said. "Not since that night."

"Wow, that's some serious blue-ball syndrome there."

He chuckled. "Masturbation can take the edge off."

Even though he was being cute by throwing my words back at me, a vision of him naked and holding himself flashed into my brain. My stomach was pressed against his groin, and I felt the log in his jeans grow exponentially. Heat rushed through me.

"Now you smell like vanilla, rum, and sex." He disengaged from me, and my throbby lady-morsels screamed, *Nooooooo*! "Which means, holding you is not a good plan. Let's focus on the case. When it's over, we can revisit this conversation. And talk about what we want to do next."

"You're right. I can't let Lily down. Finding her brother's killer has to be my number one priority." I turned myself toward the center island because my nipples were as hard as his Johnson, and looking at him only made it worse. "The case. What do you have?"

He opened a manila folder with newspaper clippings dating twenty years. "Over the past two decades, there have been some strange things going on in Paradise."

When I raised my brow, he added, "Stranger than usual. These articles are mostly about natural disasters. Tornadoes, severe lightning storms, hail…"

"The size of softballs." The unusual weather patterns captured my attention. "That is unusual." I spread the clippings out, organizing the stories by year. The disasters seemed to happen in a pattern. Initially, the storms were not so bad, but it appeared as if they had been getting progressively more devastating over the past ten years. "It looks like there is a break between September and December, then there are freak weather patterns every three months. January. March. June." I remembered how rough the town looked when I drove in. "Was there a recent storm?"

"A high-wind situation blew through town. It knocked a bunch of shingles off roofs, ruined a lot of store signs, and turned over a few trailers."

In one of the clippings, there was a picture of a collapsed house. The headline read, "Local Family Killed by Storm." I used my phone to magnify the image for a better look and noticed someone had scratched an H on the door. "There," I said, pointing to the letter.

"I see it." Ford smoothed his beard.

I groaned.

He smiled.

"Stop that." I was glad we were getting along, and I was definitely interested in exploring the possibilities, but work first. "I saw that same letter at Boyd's house scratched into his dresser, and again, I saw it scratched into the dash on Danny's car."

"What do you think it means?"

"At first, I thought it might be an initial or the start of a word that Danny and Boyd had managed to leave as a clue to their killer, but now I'm not sure. It seems less likely the victims drew the letter and more possible it was left by the murderer. Do you think it's a calling card?"

Ford tilted his head sideways and looked at the photo again. "Like a serial killer?"

"In almost every single one of these weather events, someone was injured or died. What if it wasn't an act of the Goddess and more an act of a maniac?"

"Who has figured out how to control the weather?" His expression was incredulous.

"More likely, the killer or killers are crafting something powerful enough to disrupt the weather."

"I don't know, Haze. Doesn't the leader of the witches frown on that kind of sorcery? I can't believe your grandmother wouldn't intervene. I know how swiftly she came down on your dad."

"The Grand Inquisitor," I corrected. "She's the witch in charge of all witches and warlocks, not a sweet old lady from *The Golden Girls*."

He smiled. "I love that show."

"Figures." I smiled back. "You're right, though. Clementine Battles wouldn't let this kind of bad magic go without intervening. All the evidence clears the use of black magic, but I have a gut feeling I can't shake." And my intuition rarely failed me.

"Maybe they are shielding it somehow."

"A shielding spell is still a spell. It would leave traces of magic. At Boyd's there was nothing. But honestly, I'm not completely sure of my powers. I didn't do well in witchcraft studies in school, and I haven't really practiced any new magic since I left town."

"How can this be magic but not magic?" Ford asked.

"That's the million-dollar question." I rifled through a few statements. "Mark Simmons said he overheard an argument between Danny and Robert Townsend. Why would Danny have cause to talk to him? Did anyone interview small animal pappy-whatever about the fight?"

Ford shook his head. "Today is the first time I'm seeing these. It doesn't look like it, though. You don't think Townsend could do something like what happened to Danny, do you? Besides, what would the alpha of the small prey therians be doing with Lily's brother?"

"Carla Wells told me she and Danny were mates. She said when she'd told her mom, her mom told her it was nonsense and not to speak of it again." I chewed the inside of my lip for a moment. "Maybe Danny wanted to get Townsend's blessing to be with Carla. She is a raccoon shifter like Townsend."

"You think he got angry enough to kill Danny?"

I shook my head. "It doesn't track. Besides, Boyd was a wereraccoon. And whoever or whatever killed him, killed Danny as well. I'd stake my reputation on it."

"How about first thing tomorrow morning I pick you up and we go talk to a certain alpha?" Ford asked.

I nodded. "You plan the best dates."

CHAPTER 13

I SLEPT TERRIBLY THAT NIGHT, tossing and turning as blobs of misshapen dead chased me around. When my alarm finally went off at six in the morning, I was both annoyed and relieved. I put on a pair of sweats and my tennis shoes, tied my hair back, and went for a run to clear my head.

I managed to get as far as next door. Joy Decker sat on her front porch weeping.

"Mrs. Decker," I said. "Can I help you?"

She wrung her hands. "No. No one can help me. I've lost my boy. I don't know how to go on."

"Again, I'm so sorry for your loss," I said. The sentiment was too inadequate to the situation, but most platitudes were. I hadn't planned on asking the Deckers more questions, at least not yet, but I pressed on because I wanted justice for Danny and Boyd, and I felt strongly the deaths were connected.

"Did Boyd ever mention something about the Arete?"

She looked up at me, her eyes dark with grief. "Like a mountain ridge?"

"I don't think so." Did Arete mean that? If they were talking about a mountain, then it wasn't something close to Paradise Falls. The closest thing we had to a mountain was Harmony Hill, and that barely qualified as a hill. "Was he having any problems with anyone?"

"I don't think so." She shook her head emphatically.

"What about Clayton Driver?"

Her eyes grew wary as anger turned her cheeks red. "Boyd did some work for him last year."

"What kind of work?'

"He didn't say, but I think it had something to do with pulling parts and such. Do you think Driver had anything to do with Boyd's death?" Her voice broke on the word. "Boyd hadn't been in contact with the man since he'd quit working out at the junkyard. Do you think he killed my son?"

"He is a person of interest is all, ma'am. I don't have any real suspects, yet. I'm just trying to gather all the facts. What about Robert Townsend?"

"What about him?" Joy asked suspiciously.

"Did Boyd interact with him much?"

"Of course," she said. "Bob is our leader. He holds a meeting every month for us."

"And he and Boyd were friendly."

"Yes," she said. "I don't like what you're implying, Hazel. Bob is a good man and a great leader. Our lives in this community were those of second-class citizens until Bob took over as alpha. He has made us equal with the witches and the larger animal shifters."

"I'm not implying anything, Mrs. Decker. Honest, I have no concrete leads. Mr. Townsend seems like a standup guy. Is there anything else you can tell me about Boyd? Anything weird leading up to his death? Any illness or symptoms of an illness?"

She paused for a moment then nodded. "He'd been getting some headaches and stomach pains of late. I figured it was the drugs. They can do weird things to a body, even with shifters."

I'd seen ibuprofen and anti-nausea pills in Danny's car. "Has anyone else you know been getting sick?"

"No," she said. "Just Boyd. It came on about two weeks ago."

"Had he been anywhere or done anything out of the ordinary leading up to his symptoms?"

"Nothing that I can think of," she said.

I nodded. "Thank you, Mrs. Decker. Again, I'm so sorry for your loss."

Lily stuck her head out of the door about the time I was getting ready to take off on a jog. She held up my phone. "Ford called you," she said. "He's going to be here in ten minutes."

Crap. The only running I got done after that was a quick sprint to the bathroom to fix my hair and throw on some fresh clothes.

Ford was right on time. I finished lacing my shoes and went outside to meet him at the curb. "Hey," I said when I got in the passenger side of his truck. Ford wore dark blue jeans, a chocolate-brown t-shirt, and he'd trimmed his beard, really showing off his chiseled jawline. Hubba-hubba. My whole body went taut with pleasure. Goddess be, that man could melt my panties.

He gave me a crooked grin. "Hey."

"Why so early?" I asked. "I thought we were going to see Townsend at eight." Not that I minded the early morning eye-candy.

"I thought we could get breakfast together."

"Sure, that sounds yummy."

"With my parents."

I gulped. "What?"

"I hope it's okay."

"Uhm, sure, they can join us."

"I'm really glad since Mom is cooking."

I resisted the urge to clutch my throat. We were going to the Baylor house for breakfast. "Is this a meet-the-parents kind of thing, because I'm not sure I'm ready for that yet. I mean, I just found out about the mating thing two days ago."

Ford laughed, and it warmed me to my toes. "It's not. My dad wanted to talk to you alone. Breakfast was his idea."

A big part of me sighed in relief, but a smaller part of me was disappointed. Even though I wasn't ready to shout anything from the rooftops, it had pleased me to think Ford was.

He slid his hand onto my thigh, sending zips and tingles to all the most inappropriate places on my body. "I'm ready, Hazel," he said as if reading my mind. "But I'm willing to wait for you to catch up."

The Baylor house was a large two-story home with a three-car garage and a manicured lawn in a fancy cul-de-sac on Azure Circle. Being the alpha bear had its perks, apparently.

The inside was just as nice as the outside. Mrs. Baylor's home looked photograph-ready for a spread in *Better Homes and Gardens*. The walls were painted in warm blues and sandy tones; midnight-blue floor-length curtains hung over the ten-foot window in the living room. The sofa and loveseat were covered in rich tapestry-type material that both invited and dared you to sit. I would check my butt for dirt before that happened.

Anita Baylor, Ford's mom, greeted me warmly. "Do come in, Hazel. I'm just about done with the last of the bacon." The scent of smoky meat competed for my attention with Ford's cinnamon and spice.

"Sounds great." Ford and I followed her into the dining room. Bryant Baylor sat at the head of an eight-foot table with ten chairs, four on each side and one each on the ends. It was already set with five plates, silverware, napkins, and such. A bowl of fried potatoes, some cheesy grits, a double stack of flapjacks, each a foot tall, a bottle of honey, and a bottle of blackberry syrup made my mouth water and my tummy rumble.

Bryant Baylor read a print newspaper while sipping coffee. Totally kicking it old school.

Ford offered me the chair next to his father, then he sat down on the other side of me. "This is quite a spread," I said. "We never had these kinds of meals at my house."

"Mom makes breakfast like this every day."

Anita walked in with a large plate of at least eight pounds of bacon. "Wow," I said. "That's like the Mecca of my religion." I resisted the urge to bow down to the plate of crispy, meaty goodness.

Ford chuckled. "Are you sure you're not a shifter masquerading as a witch?"

The cinnamon scent spiked. I blushed and nudged him with my elbow.

When Anita sat down on the other side of Bryant, he folded his paper, put it down on the floor then leaned over to kiss her. "Breakfast looks wonderful, sweetheart. You are a marvel."

Aww. That was sweet! My face must have reflected my thoughts because Ford nudged me.

"Where's Lincoln?" Anita asked.

"Not down, yet," Bryant said.

I almost ducked for cover when Anita roared, "Lincoln! Get your furry butt downstairs now!"

"I'm coming!" roared back a male voice.

Bryant smiled at his wife before his face turned serious and we locked gazes. "Agent Kinsey."

"Call me, Hazel."

He nodded. "Hazel. I'm afraid I agree with you about the coalition hiding something. If you are serious about wanting to find out about what happened to Danny, and frankly, what's been happening to our town for the past thirty years, you need to talk to your father."

"Why?"

He gave me a meaningful look. "I know my son shared those newspaper clippings with you. Who do you think gave them to him? When your father went to jail, the disasters and deaths stopped for a brief period of time, then they started back up again, but the gruesome death of Daniel Mason, and now Boyd Decker, happened after he arrived back in town. Clementine Battles insisted he be put back on the council, but it's the one thing I agreed with Adele Adams about. That man has no business being in charge of anything going on in this town."

"That man is my father," I said. Why in the heck was I defending him? It wasn't like I disagreed with Bryant about my dad being on the coalition. However, I found it a bitter pill to swallow that he might be somehow involved in the death of my best friend's brother. Hell, Lily spent a lot of time at our house. My dad wouldn't do that, would he?

He killed Mom, I reminded myself.

"I'll ask him," I finally said, after I'd processed the information. "I don't want to believe it, but you're right, it's a possibility."

A boy, nearly as tall at Ford and looking very similar to the high school boy I sloppy-kissed all those years ago, stomped into the room. He flopped into the seat next to his mom. "I don't know why I got to get up this early on a Sunday. It's bad enough five days a week," he complained. Then he noticed me. His temperamental expression turned to chagrinned. Having a sulk-filled pity party in front of a stranger had taken the vinegar out of him.

"Hazel," Anita said. "This brooding young man is our son Lincoln. I was pregnant with him when you and Ford graduated."

I nodded to the kid. "Nice to meet you, Lincoln."

"Is this Ford's new girlfriend?" the teenager asked.

Before I could jump in with a big ol' maybe, Ford's dad said, "Special Agent Kinsey is here investigating the terrible things in our town. Show some respect."

"Yes, sir," the kid mumbled then stabbed his fork into a stack of the pancakes. "Pass the bacon," he muttered next.

After breakfast, I resisted the urge to unbutton the top button on my jeans. Lincoln went back upstairs to do whatever it was teenage boys did on Sunday mornings. I took the opportunity to speak more with Bryant Baylor while Ford helped his mother clearing the table and cleaning the dishes. If I hadn't already been gaga for the guy, seeing him clean and oil a cast iron skillet would have done the trick.

"Mr. Baylor, is there anyone else on the coalition that you find suspicious?" After all, my witchy radar had pinged on everyone but Mary the cat queen.

"There isn't a one of them I would trust as far as I can throw them. They are always making moves for more power for the folks they represent, which is what they are supposed to do, but as the *ursa* for my people, I have to be vigilant that we don't lose our standing in the process."

"Anyone more power hungry than the rest?" I asked.

"I would put Adele Adams at the top. Your grandmother will have her hands full if Adele's magic gets much stronger. The woman has become very powerful with age."

"It's unusual, but it happens." I nodded. "Thanks. I appreciate the information. If you think of anything else, please call me." I dug a card out of my purse and handed it to him. "And thank you for talking to me this morning."

"Uh hum," he said. He picked up his paper from the floor, flicked it open, and effectively concluded our conversation.

Ford poked his head into the room. "You ready, Hazel?" Cinnamon frosted the room. Sort of like a witch and a bear shifter catching each other's scent. Oy.

"Sure," I said.

Anita bustled past him. She gave me an unexpected hug and said, "You come back anytime."

"If you keep making breakfast like that," I told her, "you won't be able to keep me away."

CHAPTER 14

WHEN WE WERE BACK on the road, Ford said, "I got a call from a contact who gave me Dennis Mitchell's location."

"The bungling detective?" I asked. "Way to bury the lead!"

"We'll stop by Wonderland Reality first, interview Robert Townsend, then we'll go hunt down Mitchell. He's the next county over in Lister."

"Sounds like a plan." I liked the hunting part. If it weren't for Mitchell's poor investigating, Danny's killer might have been caught already, and the poor Deckers would not be suffering now. I planned to make that bad cop pay for it.

It took only five minutes to get to Wonderland Reality. Robert Townsend wasn't in his office when we got there at eight-thirty in the morning. His secretary, Sally Teeter, a dark-haired woman of average build, told us he'd taken a personal day.

"Do you know why?"

"I don't," she said. "It was personal." A small smile formed on her lips, happy with her own cleverness. "He'll be back in tomorrow. Are you two looking to buy a home?"

Before I could throw out a gazillion denials because of my insecurity, Ford said, "Why, yes, we are."

Sally nodded as she looked Ford up and down. "I know Bob's got a couple of properties that would suit a big fella like yourself," she said. I looked at the board on the wall behind her with property listings. There were as many commercial buildings as personal homes…and trailers.

"Did he sell Daniel Mason a trailer about eight months ago?"

"He did," Sally said brightly, then shook her head. "Poor kid. Terrible thing that happened to him. He seemed like he was doing better. Sometimes you just can't dig yourself out of the holes you create."

"No one can dig themselves out of a hole," Ford said. "It just gets deeper."

Sally nodded. "Exactly."

There were framed pictures on the wall of Townsend on vacation in what looked like the Caribbean, Germany, Italy, because he was standing to the side like he was pushing over the Leaning Tower of Pisa, Ireland with a Guinness, England, leaning on a rock at Stonehenge, in Paris squishing the Eiffel Tower, and a few other places I didn't recognize. Weirdly, he was alone in every photograph.

On another wall was a collage of Townsend with local people standing outside of properties, proudly displaying "Sold" signs. I recognized two people in one of the many pictures. It was my parents, my mother thick in the belly with me, and they were standing outside the house I grew up in. My father had known Townsend for a long time. Maybe this was something both of them were doing together. I still wished I knew what was going on.

Before I could ask Sally if she knew if my father and Townsend were cold-blooded killers, Ford's phone rang.

He looked at me. "It's the station. I have to take this." He answered. "Officer Baylor." His brow pinched, creating deep frown lines. "I understand. I'll be right out." He hung up.

"What is it?"

"There's another body."

"Where?"

He rubbed the crease between his eyes. "Junkyard Dog."

"Oh, crap."

"Yep," he said. "You want to come along?"

"What about Nichols? Won't you get in trouble?"

"He's an ass."

"But he's a boss ass. I don't want your life to get harder because I'm back in town."

"Since you've arrived back in town, everything's harder." His blue eyes twinkled. "Are you coming or not?"

"Not yet." I gave his package a quick glance. "But we can save that for later. Right now, we have a crime scene to get to."

I heard Sally sigh as we exited. "Honeymooners," she said wistfully.

On the drive out to the junkyard, I saw I had two missed calls from Lily. I must have turned off the ringer by accident.

"You should call her," Ford said as if reading my mind.

"Thank you, Dr. Phil."

He shrugged. "Or not."

I put my phone away. My head had forgiven Lily, and I never wanted her to know just how hard this was for me, but my heart wasn't ready. My father being in town was an unexpected blow. He killed my mom. He wiped her from the face of the Earth. This is something I'd want to freaking know about. And now…was he really a monster?

"Did you know my dad was back?"

"Yes." He gripped the steering wheel tighter. "My father mentioned it when he arrived in town. I didn't know you didn't know, though, or I would have said."

The gravel road out to Junkyard Dog was hazy with dust and debris. Two marked police cars, along with a silver sedan, a blue full-sized pickup, and a green and yellow compact truck were parked along the drive. My heart froze a beat. "Oh no." I unsnapped my seat belt as Ford parked. "No, no, no."

"What is it, Haze?"

"That's Lily's truck." I yanked on the handle and threw my body at the door to open it. "That's Lily's," I said again. I could hear Ford telling me to wait, but I couldn't. What if the dead person was…

I brushed the awful thought from my head as I sprinted for the metal building where a small crowd had gathered.

Chief Nichols' eyes widened at my speedy approach. He held his hand up in the universal sign for halt. I brushed past him without slowing down. Inside, the overwhelming scent of rot and decay nearly sent me to my knees. I gagged at the stench but kept going. Where Danny's Chevelle had been on the lift, now there was something that looked like a bloated bag of blood. There wasn't enough light for me to tell for sure.

I scanned the room for any sign of Lily. Something to tell me that she wasn't involved.

Red fur wrapped around my neck as Tizzy unexpectedly flew in for a landing on my shoulder.

"I can't find Lily. Is that…" I pointed to the dripping object on the lift. "Could it be?"

"No," Tizzy said. "Lily got a call to come here, and that was already up there." She rubbed her cheek against mine as if for her own comfort, which meant she found the scene as disturbing as I did. "Apparently, it's a guy named Dennis Mitchell."

"The detective in charge of Danny's case."

"If you say so, Haze."

Ten kinds of relief flooded me. It was too bad for Dennis Mitchell. No one deserved to end up like that, but I was more grateful than words could say that it wasn't my best friend. "Did you ride with Lily?"

"Yes. She tried to call you."

Guilt pinched me. "My ringer was off."

"Uh huh." She whacked me in the side of the face with her bushy tail. "Lily and I got here half an hour ago. She was talking to that asshole Frank, and I came in here for a closer look. When I went back out to find her, she was gone."

"And Frank?"

"Him too."

I took my phone out and dialed her number. Straight to voicemail. I had two voicemails from her, so I dialed my messages next.

Message One: *Hey, Haze. This is Lily. Duh. Right. You know that already. Anyhow. Got a call from the Dick Knuckles. He's asked me to come out to Junkyard Dog. Not sure why, but I wanted you to know since Tiz is coming with me.*

Message Two: *Hey. It's me again.* Her voice was tight as she continued. *Dennis Mitchell is dead. Someone said I threatened him for bungling Danny's case. Dear Goddess, Haze. I'm a suspect.* I heard a man say, *Can I talk to you a minute?* Then Lily said, *Okay, Haze. I've got to go. Call me.*

My guilt compounded. "I need to find Lily."

"I'm sure she's around here somewhere, Haze," Tizzy said, but she didn't sound convinced.

"Special Agent Kinsey," Nichols said as he walked up behind me. "This is not the Daniel Mason case, so I'll ask you to quit contaminating my crime scene."

Clayton Driver was right behind him, his arms crossed over his chest.

I pushed past him. "Where's Danny's car?"

"Wha—I don't know what you mean?" Driver pretended ignorance.

"When did you discover the—" I waved at the thing in the air.

"I'm the only one allowed to ask questions around here, young lady."

"Fine," I said. "Don't help me." I pushed past both men.

I blanked on a spell so threw out:

"Double bubble. Show me trouble.

Show me what Mitchell could see.

Point to the clues, so mote it be."

Several spots began to glow for me. I walked to the first. A puddle of tarry liquid, too dark for blood, was pooled near the victim. The second spot behind the lift and near the acetylene torch had an *H* scratched into the concrete floor, but like a small pimple on a friend's face, I wouldn't have noticed it if the spell hadn't pointed it out.

I knelt next to it and traced the symbol with my finger. "What the heck are you?"

"That's a hagalaz." Tanya Geller stood over me, peering down at the mark.

"A what-a-laz?"

"It's a rune of disruption." She squinched her perky nose. "It's Witchcraft 101, Hazel."

"I flunked that class." I stood up and dusted my hand on my pants. "I've seen the same mark in relation to Danny Mason and Boyd Decker. I think having it show up again is more than a coincidence."

"It's usually half of a spell. The rune is rarely used alone." She put her hand close to it. "It's not active."

Under the acetylene torch machine, something grew so bright I couldn't ignore it. I reached under the welder and pulled out a sphere with many points coming out of it. It looked like an ice crystal, but I was certain it was made of glass.

The prism in Danny's car, the faceted glass ball in Boyd's room, and now this star-like ornament.

"Looks like a tree ornament," Tanya said.

It didn't feel like magic, but neither did the rune. It should, right?

Clayton Driver grabbed me by the forearm and leaned in close. "If you know what's good for you, you'll back off, Miss FBI."

I staggered sideways, eyes wide in disgust and disbelief. "Let go of me before I shoot off your fingers." Magic flared along my arm where he clasped me, and he jerked his hand away.

In the next second, Ford was next to me and glaring at Driver.

He raised his eyebrow and chuckled. "Be careful when looking for answers, Agent Kinsey. You might just find them."

I looked over to Ford. "Was that a threat?"

He growled. "I think it was."

"What are you doing here, Baylor? It's your day

off," Nichols said. "And what are you doing here with Kinsey?"

"Leta Givens called me, Chief. I figured you'd want some extra help working the scene."

I remembered Givens. She was the desk officer at the station. So, the chief hadn't called Ford. While Nichols was distracted with Ford, I took matters into my own hands. Lily was missing, and right now, she was the only body I was interested in, and I wanted to find her alive and well.

I stroked my familiar's head. "Show me where you last saw her, Tiz."

The squirrel hopped off my shoulder and raced for the exit. I exchanged a look with Ford then followed at a brisk pace after her.

"Wait a minute, Mizz Kinsey," Chief Nichols said.

I snapped my fingers at him, surprising myself and him when a jolt of electricity flared from my fingertips. "It's Special Agent Kinsey, Dick Knuckles. And I'll thank you to remember that from now on."

Ford stepped in front of him, blocking Nichols' view of me as I headed out. I heard him say something along the lines of, "Can I get a word with you, Chief?" The menace in the brilliant bear's tone came across loud and clear.

With my obstacle out of the way, I hurried to catch up to my familiar.

CHAPTER 15

TIZZY LEAPED into the air and swished her tail in a fanning wave to get my attention near a row of stacked smashed cars. When I got close enough, she said, "They were chatting right here."

I let my fear form a spell.

"Goddess don't let this be the end.
Show me the path to find my friend.
Protect her and keep her safe for me.
This is my prayer, so mote it be."

Footsteps lit up a path that led down the row.

"What's happening, Haze? Did it work?"

"Yes," I said, concentrating on following the glowing marks.

"Really?" She took two giant leaps toward me and clambered up my clothes until she was in her favorite spot. "I don't see anything? Are you sure it's working? I've heard stress can make you delusional."

"Stop talking, Tiz." The path continued on past the walls of dead cars to the back fence. There was an opening in the chain link that was haphazardly covered with a piece of wood. The steps were scattered, and I saw the glowing outline of a body being dragged through. "Oh, Goddess."

"What? What!"

"I think Lily is unconscious."

"Are you sure *you're* not unconscious?" she chattered nervously in my ear, something she did when her anxiety levels rose. "I want to believe you, Haze, but you were never much good at spell work. I still have a few places where my fur doesn't grow well to prove it."

"Trust me, Tiz. This is the one kind of spell I know how to work." I picked up the board, and we crawled through the fence. The tracks glowed across the field for as far as I could see. The phone call message had come in more than forty minutes earlier. I worried Lily didn't have the time it would take me to cover the area on foot. "I'm going to try a transport spell."

"Dear Goddess, kill me now," she prayed.

"You were complaining that you wished I'd used one."

"Because I knew you wouldn't!" she chirped. "You're going to turn me wrong side up and inside out."

"That is a risk," I agreed without any real conviction. I was pretty sure I could get us from one place to the other unharmed. I just wasn't sure *where* we would end up. "You can stay here."

"And let you have all the fun? No way. Besides, I'm spoiling to skin that rotten beaver for his cheap shot. The side of my head still smarts." She clung to me like her life depended on it. "Do eet!"

I took a deep breath and crossed my fingers. Desperation brought the words. I could only hope I didn't say something that would land me in a lava pit.

"Goddess show us the path's end.

Help us find our in-need friend.

Transport us far across this land.

Hold us safely in your hand.

Please don't put us up a tree.

Transport us now, so mote it be."

Tizzy snickered in my ear. "You're really bad at poetr-eeeeeee!" Her squeal ended when we blinked out. When we blinked back into existence, it continued. "Eeeeeeee! What the fading hell?"

We were not on the other side of an open field. Instead, we'd landed in some small, dark room.

Tizzy sneezed. "There's so much dust!"

"Where are we?"

"It's your stupid spell," Tiz hissed. "Make a light, Haze."

"I'd blow this place up." Probably. I fumbled around until my fingers alighted on a handle. I turned it and opened a door. A small amount of light poured in, and I could see we were in some kind of storage closet.

A thin layer of white powder coated Tiz's fur, my hair, and my shirt. "What is this?" I touched it. It felt smooth and silky. "Some kind of powder. Maybe concrete silt."

Tizzy coughed and hacked then examined her paws. "At least I still have all ten of my fingers. Damn, Haze. You chipped my manicure."

Voices carried like a murmuring brook to our location. "Shhhh. I hear something."

"I'm not deaf," Tizzy whispered. "I hear them too."

Quietly, we eased the door open enough to look outside. There was six feet of concrete floor in front of us with a staircase that went down. I crouched and made my way to the edge.

Down below, I saw Adele Adams and Frank Leggert in a wide open space with a thick, gnarled tree growing up through the center of the floor.

Adele was working with Frank? It seemed too odd to be true.

I stifled a gasp when I saw Clayton Driver carry Lily into the room like she was a sack of flour. How in the hell had he gotten here so fast? He was a

154

shifter. It wasn't like he could fast-travel like a witch. Adele must've used magic to get her cohort to the warehouse. It was the only scenario that made sense. My stomach churned as Clayton put her back against the tree and held her there while Frank started tying her to the trunk with a rope.

My hand instantly went to my gun, but it found nothing. Cripes! I'd left it in my purse. The purse that I'd left in Ford's truck. My phone was in my pocket. I pulled it out to text Ford, but it dawned on me that I had no idea where the hell I was at. Goddess-damn transport spell.

I heard Lily moan, and my body went cold.

"Oh, Haze," Tiz said in my ear, her voice full of trepidation. "Do something."

Adele was an old witch with super witchy powers. I could barely manage a simple relocation spell. How was I supposed to take her down without a weapon? "I'm thinking."

"I thought I saw smoke," she quipped. "Quit thinking and start doing."

The windows on this upper level were dirty, some were even broken. Since I couldn't discern any real utility for the building, I made the assumption it was abandoned. I couldn't know for sure whether Frank had driven here with Lily, but I knew that Clayton had been at the crime scene when I got there. He most likely drove. But how far? The transportation spell felt like it had lasted only a few seconds, but what if it had taken longer?

I pulled up Ford's phone number in messaging and texted: *In an abandoned building. Unsure where. Unarmed. Adams, Driver, Leggert here. Lily hostage. Weird-ass tree in the middle of an empty warehouse-like first floor. Find me.*

Dear Goddess let that be enough information for him to get here in time.

"Now what?" Tizzy whispered.

"How stupid are you, Frank?" Clayton Driver yelled. He poked a finger in Frank's narrow chest. "I swear to the Goddess that beavers are the dumbest creatures."

"Shut your mouth, Clayton," Adele said. "Don't be evoking the *you know who* in here." When he gave her a blank stare, she said, "Starts with a G. Ends with an S."

"Oh...right."

Adele shook her head, her blonde hair flouncing around her shoulders. Clayton looked at her like a kid starved for candy. It appeared she was using something other than her magical powers to keep him on a leash. "Bringing the Mason girl here was stupid. As long as she's missing, that bitch Hazel Kinsey won't stop digging around."

Clayton snarled. "Then we'll take care of her, too."

Adele slapped him. He growled, but she held her hand up, a fireball forming in her palm. "Try me, cat."

He backed down.

"We can't touch the Kinsey girl. She is under the Grand Inquisitor's protection. Dammit! The girl showed no promise as a child. Even her mother thought she'd amount to nothing better than a slight step up from a human. But I believe now that she carries more raw magic than I've seen in a long time."

Ouch. That hurt. Adele had known my mother?

Wait. She thought I had a lot of raw magic?

"Priscilla was key in these rituals." She paced in front of the two shifters. "Maybe you aren't so dumb for grabbing the werecougar."

She touched Lily's hair, and I focused my thoughts on burning her face off.

Nothing happened. So much for raw, untapped power.

"We can use Hazel's friend to get her to help finish the spell. And this time, Kent won't be able to interfere."

What? I was seriously struggling to process Adele's revelations. Had my mother been a powerful evil witch, and my dad had stopped her somehow? If that were true, he wouldn't have gotten thrown into witch jail, right? He'd cast a bond-severing spell that was above his pay grade and caused my mom to disappear from the world entirely. At least, that's the story I'd been told.

I gestured to Tizzy to get down from my shoulder. She jumped to the floor and waited. "Stay here," I mouthed. She nodded once.

CHAPTER 16

THE STAIRS WERE CONCRETE, easy to descend without making a lot of noise. I had to stop this somehow. I could use Adele's misconception that I might have some of my mother's gifts to an advantage.

Frank Leggert snickered when Lily groaned again. What had they done to knock her out?

The drugs. Both Boyd and Danny had recreational amounts of opiates in their system, but what if they hadn't taken it willingly? That would explain the drugs in Danny's system after Carla had sworn he'd been clean. It might take an elephant's dose to put a shifter out, and by the time the bad stuff started the drug would be wearing off.

Why hadn't I seen it before?

"I know how we can get Hazel Kinsey here and helping," Clayton said.

Adele gave him an appraising look. "How?"

Clayton reached back, grabbed Lily's arm and with one quick jerk, he snapped it. The crack echoed against the walls.

Lily screamed, suddenly alert.

"Stop!" I shouted. "Please don't hurt her."

Clayton smiled. "Just like that."

He'd known I was there. How?

"I'm a werecougar, Agent Kinsey. Unlike the beaver here, I have a nose, I have ears, and I have eyes."

"Hey," Frank said. "I have eyes."

"Shut up, Frank," Adele and Clayton said simultaneously.

Crap. Fifteen years of working with humans, I'd forgotten how attuned shifters were to their senses.

"So glad you could join us, Hazel," Adele said. I didn't like her pleased tone. "Why don't you come on down and join the party."

Clayton poked Lily's arm. She cried out. "Don't keep us waiting."

I swore to the Goddess I was going fry his furry ass. As I walked the last ten steps to the floor, I asked, "How has the Grand Inquisitor not caught wind of your foul magic? Have you figured out a way to shield your powers against her?"

Adele laughed. It was lyrical and lovely, and it

made me want to barf. "Clementine can sit on Stonehenge and spin." She laughed again.

"Stonehenge?" Townsend's photographs. Had Adele been the one taking the pictures? Had they been in on it together all along? My gut said yes. An awful idea came to me. Stonehenge…

Oh, Goddess. Was Adele really dabbling in… "You're practicing druid magic."

Her eyes widened. "You are definitely smarter than you look. Your mother would be proud."

"I don't understand why you're doing all this, Adele. You're a powerful witch already."

"But not the *most* powerful." She shook her head. "And once I harness your energy for the final spell, I will be." Adele gave me haughty look. "Clementine will bow to me."

Adele was jealous with a capital J. "So, you've been learning druid spells to become more powerful than the Grand Inquisitor? To what purpose?"

The blonde witch shrugged. "Clementine has her kingdom. Now I want it to be mine."

"And my mother was helping you?"

"Oh, darling girl," Adele said, syrup thick in her words. "All of this was your mother's idea."

This little nugget of information took the wind right out of my sails. "Liar."

"Not in this case."

Frank and Clayton laughed.

I threw my rage at them, lightning bolts shooting from my hands. I struck Frank in the leg. He went down like a screaming beaver-man with a large charred hole in his thigh. The second bolt bounced off a force field.

I turned on Adele. She held her hand out, casting a protective bubble around Clayton.

"You can have Frank, but Clayton is my pet." Her eyes glowed with green as a red light bathed her skin. A fireball skimmed my shoulder as I took a diving roll toward the tree. I put myself between Lily and the scary-ass witch-druid.

"If you hurt Lily, I'll never help you."

A tall man with black hair walked into the room, confirming my suspicions. He looked surprised to see me, but his face remained cool and impassive.

"Ease up, Adele. We need Hazel more than we need her friend's pain," the raccoon shifter said as he ran his hand through his neatly styled hair. "Hello, Agent Kinsey. So nice to see you again."

Well, screw me blue, the *raton* really *was* a stinking rat. "Why? Why would you help her?"

He held out his hand to Adele, and she took it. Robert smiled. "You misunderstand what's going on here, Hazel. I'm not helping Adele. She's helping *me*."

"Pentagram on a popsicle stick," I said. "I did not see this coming."

"We are the Arete," he said. "I can no longer sit by and let my people be subjugated to witches and every large shifter that wants to keep us in our place. The only way to take power is to be powerful." He cupped Adele's cheek, and she crooned. "Addy and I have similar goals."

Yuck. "You are completely nuts." I thought about what Adele had said about my mother. "And what about Mom? Had she wanted power, too?"

"Not at first," Adele said. "But druid magic is seductive, and we can practice without anyone knowing. I had thought she was insane when she first brought me the idea, but after Bob and I went to England and experienced the potential, a magic that both witches and shifters could use, we got on board."

"But you had to destroy parts of the town. Kill people to make it work. That can be worth it?"

Townsend lifted his arms and began to wave his hands around in front of him. I thought he might be having a seizure for a moment until the symbols began appearing in the air. I recognized the H.

"Hagalaz."

"Very good. It took me a long time without your mother to master using the rune without bringing down the wrath of nature." He held up a piece of cut glass. "It was a matter of infusing some baubles with a druid spell for temperance and pairing the two.

The last three sacrifices have proven we're almost there."

"Almost where?"

"Our own Utopia, of course."

"You've been sniffing the glue too long." Paradise Failed, once again. "You won't get away with this."

"There is nothing you can do, Hazel," Adele said. "I'm not breaking any witch rules."

"You are breaking every rule of common decency, and killing is against all laws, you smug lunatic."

She glared at me, anger aging her face. "Sticks and stones will break Lily's bones, but names will make me hurt you." She flung another ball of fire at me. I screamed as the burning pitch hit my forearm.

"We need her," Robert said.

"She'll never help, my love. Can't you see? She is stalling."

Lily was in and out of it. The pain burning through the opiates in her system.

I said quickly:

"Bound be unbound, Goddess hear me.
Release my friend, so mote it be."

The ropes that had been wrapped around Lily dropped to the ground, and she crumpled to the floor. The witch and the three craphead shifters stared at me with abject surprise. They couldn't have been more amazed than I was. I couldn't believe the spell worked!

"Silence her!" Townsend commanded. "Don't let her attract the Lady G."

"Goddess," I shouted. "Goddess hear me."

Another fireball flew at me. I countered with a lightning bolt that Adele easily deflected.

A high-pitched screech made everyone look up.

Tizzy, arms spread, wings flapping, glided down on us like a red, hairy angel of death. She hit Adele in the face then jumped on top of Robert before leaping into another gravity-defying glide to where I stood.

"I'm with you, Haze."

The pride when I looked down at my fierce familiar made my chest swell until it forced tears from my eyes. I stared down Adele.

"Goddess help me scratch this itch.

Give me strength to beat this bitch."

Emerald-green flames poured over me as my aura filled with an energy so powerful, I thought it would explode me. I released the magic in one giant lightning bolt that headed straight for Adele. She tried to block it, but her druid magic was no match.

A split second before it could zap her, Robert Townsend threw a giant mountain lion in the lightning's path. The cougar blew up like a microwaved turkey wrapped in foil.

Goddess, I'd just whacked Clayton Driver. "Noooo!" My fury wasn't sated. I threw another bolt, and this time, the beaver got it. The room reeked of singed fur.

The green flames were fading. I was losing energy. Townsend started rune casting on the air again, and Adele was bathed in green, red, blue, and yellow flames.

"Crap, we're screwed," Tizzy yipped. Then said with a little too much excitement, "Now that Frank's dead, do you think Colleen is free?"

"Not the time, Tiz." She really did have beaver fever.

"Right!" She scampered back behind me.

The flames were burning out fast. I could take one last shot at Adele or try to save my friend. I chose my friend. I focused my energy on creating a protective bubble for Tizzy and Lily. As Adele's magical blaze burned brighter and thicker than any I'd ever seen, it sounded like a freight train gaining steam.

"Save yourself, Haze," Lily yelled over the noise. She was awake now and cradling her broken arm. "Don't die for me."

"Forget it, Lily," I shouted as the protective bubble firmed into place. "I'm not going to desert you. Not again."

A side door to the building blew in. I nearly faltered in my protection spell when I saw Ford run into the room, his face full of rage-y determination.

Adele turned on him.

"No!" I shouted as a tremendous fireball sailed at him.

My father, Kent Kinsey, knocked Ford sideways, and Chief Nichols, who'd run in after my father, threw up a protection spell.

It wasn't enough. Adele's power had grown too strong for the warlock. When the bubble burst, so did Nichols.

Dear Goddess. Warlock goo flew everywhere. I gagged. Adele gagged. I guess the art of torturing people had done nothing to harden that reflex.

Ford and my dad ran to my side. A worthless witch, a brooding bear, an unreliable warlock, a horny squirrel, and a broken cougar. The Fab Five we weren't, but knowing I wasn't fighting alone gave me courage.

The strong scent of snickerdoodles eased the fear building inside me. "I'm with you, Hazel. I will stand and fight by your side no matter what." Ford squeezed my hand. I was amazed at how clearly I'd heard him over the hullabaloo of chaos magic. He let go of my hand and turned into a giant grizzly bear. He roared at the raccoon shifter and his psycho witch girlfriend, the sound vibrating the air.

"We have to cut the binds that tie Adele to the tree," my dad yelled, as the freight train of the witch's magic grew louder.

"How? It's not like we can see them?"

"Can't we?" he asked.

As a famous real estate tycoon once said, it was all about location, location, location.

I focused my power at Adele.

"Ties that bind this tree to thee.

Reveal yourself so all can see.

The ties that bind, so mote it be."

A long, glowing tether slithering around the tree's roots flowed out across the room and speared straight through Robert Townsend's chest, out his back, and into the flames consuming Adele. She gathered another large ball of nuclear flames in her arms. A vision of all of us ending up like Nichols made me shudder.

"Whatever you have planned, Dad, you better do it quick!"

Dad wiggled his fingers:

"Tree of Blood, Witch of Lies.

Slice away your mortal ties.

Earth. Water. Fire. Air.

Sever bonds to this earthly lair."

The flames around Adele spiked. Robert Townsend tried to run, but Ford the bear leaped the distance, smashing him down with his massive paws. Next, he tore off Townsend's head, and the *raton* was no more. Unfortunately, that still left

Adele, and her power seemed to be going atomic-bomb dangerous.

"Ford! Run!" The bear took one look at the witch as her flames went supernova and barreled his way toward me. I turned to my dad. "Uh, I think you maybe made it worse!"

"It should have worked."

Ford, a massive man again, only naked now, took me in his arms and kissed me. A last act of love before dying. Hubba.

A sonic BOOM shook the entire building, and I looked up in time to get hit in the shoulder with a piece of charred meat. "Ew!"

The silence following the boom was deafening. My dad picked up Lily and carried her over the battle-field of body parts. I couldn't remember the last time I'd been proud to be his daughter. My eyes misted.

"I'm proud to have you for a mate." Ford's gaze softened as he brushed a stray swatch of bloody skull and hair from my arm.

"So gross," I said.

"It really is." His blue eyes alighted around the room. "I've seen it before with guys like Townsend."

"What?"

"Small mammal syndrome."

I grinned. "You did not just go there."

He laughed, and it made me feel good to my toes.

"Proud to be my mate, huh?" I covered his freed willy with my torso.

"Don't make me take it back." He lifted me into his arms. "You have a decision to make."

"Don't forget about me!" Tizzy scaled his leg and settled into my lap. "Nothing like bear-to-door service."

"Not so fast."

The voice froze us all in place. Standing in the middle of the mess, in an immaculate white dress suit and white gloves, her silver hair neatly slicked back in a rolled bun, was none other than my grandma, the Grand Inquisitor herself.

"Hello, Mother," my dad said.

"You missed all the fireworks," I said, kind of pissed that she hadn't shown up sooner.

She rolled her eyes so far back they turned white. "You're a riot." She curled her gloved fist on her hip. "Is this Adele Adams?" She pointed at barbecued body parts.

I shrugged. "Some of it." The pile of goo near the door was my biggest regret. "Too bad about Chief Nichols. I would have bet my savings he was one of the bad guys. Color me surprised."

"He was a dick," Ford said. "But you're right. He wasn't evil. Just incompetent."

"Agreed," my dad said. "Are you satisfied now, Grand Inquisitor?"

"You've done well, Kent. I will allow that the death of your wife was an accident of her own making." She pulled off one glove and glanced around at the meat explosion. "Adele has always been a jealous witch. Even as a child, I knew she'd be trouble." She puffed up a breath of air that rustled her bangs. "Family. Can't live with them. Can't kill them." She winked at me. "Sometimes a little help is needed in that department."

"She is a member of our family?"

"A very distant cousin." She examined her long, neatly manicured nails on the hand not wearing the glove before turning her all-knowing gaze on me. "You owe me a favor, Hazel Marie Kinsey."

I didn't like that she had invoked my entire name. "Killing Adele wasn't favor enough?"

She shrugged. "Fine. We'll call that favor number one. But, as you may recall, we agreed on two favors."

"Right, right. So mote it be."

"Why do you keep adding that to your spells?" my father asked. "Not judging. Just asking."

"I thought…you mean you don't have to?" I wasn't about to tell them about my *Witchcraft for Idiots* book. "But the Grand Inquisitor said it to me when we made the deal."

She shrugged. "You believed in the words. Belief gives the magic power."

"Awesome." I felt like a total dummy.

"Don't be ashamed, Hazel. You are very strong, and you will do great things for this town."

Ford's arms tightened on me.

"I haven't decided…"

"Now you're being a dummy," she said. "You will be the new chief of police. I'm ordering it so." She pierced me with her or-I'll-smite-you stare. "No arguing."

"I don't know…" I looked up at Ford. "Would it make you mad if I were your boss?"

"You mean you want to stay in Paradise Falls?"

"I really do."

"Then it would not make me mad." He kissed me, squishing Tizzy between us. She squeaked her protest. "I don't want to leave, and I don't want to live without you. It's a win."

"Hello, injured BFF over here," Lily crooned. "I really need to get to Dr. Geller."

"She's a medical examiner," I protested. Uck. I didn't want that bear-flirting bitch fixing my friend. "She works with dead people."

"She's the only doctor in town," Lily countered. She held her arm to her chest. "I can heal a lot, but that jerk broke the bone clean in half."

The Grand Inquisitor clapped her hands. "I will take the werecougar to a top-notch healer. She will fix her right up." She clapped her hands again, and

Lily disappeared from my father's arms. Grandmother's eyes softened for a moment, and she uncharacteristically put a comforting hand on my cheek. "Don't worry, Hazel. She's in good hands now. Goodbye, Granddaughter."

"Good—" And my grandmother was gone before I could say bye.

CHAPTER 17

AFTER HE SET ME DOWN, I stared into Ford's blue eyes mostly to avoid looking around at all the people parts. "I can't believe it's over."

"You were pretty damn spectacular."

His compliment made me squishy in all my squishy places. I wiggled against him, and his timber hardened against me. He growled. I grinned.

"Get some, Haze!" Tizzy said.

I blushed. Sometimes it was easy to forget about the tiny squirrel in the room.

The soft noise of a throat clearing got my attention. My dad stood alone, his hands by his side, his palms open.

Goddess on toast. I'd rubbed a naked guy in front of my father.

"Haze," he said. "I'm sorry."

I'd blamed him for so long, it was hard to get a grip on how to feel now that I knew he didn't kill my mother. At least, not on purpose. "How come you never told me you were innocent? That Mom was the one practicing bad magic?"

"I wanted to protect you. Besides, it was hard to convince the Grand Inquisitor, my own mother, I hadn't killed Priscilla on purpose. I believed that without proof, I'd never convince you, either." He shook his head. "I wasn't a perfect father, even before I tried to sever the pair bond with your mom. But I do love you."

Ford let me go, and I went to my dad and hugged him. "We'll get through this."

He hugged me back. "Danny died because he got too close to the truth. Lily deserves to know. Her brother died an honorable death. His and Lily's parents were victims of Adele, Robert, and your mom. I suspected but couldn't prove the crime. It's why they killed him."

"Why break all his bones?"

"Pain," Dad said. "The more pain that fed the spell, the more powerful the magic. Druidic magic is more potent with sacrifice."

"And Boyd?"

"I think because he and Danny were friends, they believed he knew more than he actually did. They killed Dennis Mitchell because he decided to blackmail them for more money after they'd bribed him to hide evidence in the investigation."

"Lily and the Deckers will sleep easier, knowing their loved ones can rest in peace now," said Ford.

I kissed Ford. Not a quick bump of lips, but a deep, meaningful, sucking-his-tongue-down-my-throat kiss.

He growled and yanked me hard against his body.

"I'm out of here," my dad said, then blinked away.

"We're covered in shifter-witch gunk," I said when Ford's hands slid under my shirt.

"The mating urge is strong." His fingers danced over my nipples, sending sharp spikes of pleasure to my hoo-ha.

"Bear and witch.

Mating itch.

Too much power.

Need a shower.

Goddess hear me.

So mote it be."

In a quick fade out then back in, we were standing in a five-foot marble shower with ten pulsating jet sprayers and an overhead rainmaker. "Oh, man, I'm getting good!"

I turned on the water and stripped my clothes while Ford tossed them over the clear door.

"Are you sure, Haze?" he asked when he had me naked with my breasts mashed up against his bare furry chest. "Mating is for life."

"Do you wish I wouldn't have kissed you the night of the party? I mean, I was a nobody in high school. I wasn't even on your radar."

"There have been times I regretted it because it's hard to be alone." He brushed back a wet strand of hair from my face. "But…you were wearing black leggings, a blue tank top, and a pair of pink ankle boots. Oh, and you wore your hair in a ponytail to the side. You were pretty adorable."

"The night of the party?"

"No," Ford said, shaking his head. "The day I asked you to pass me the catsup."

"Oh." I blinked. "Oh."

He growled as he lifted me off the floor of the shower, my feet dangling as he pressed his forehead to mine. "You were on my radar, Hazel Kinsey. Then and now."

"Yes," I told Ford. "Let's make this work."

"It's for life." He smiled. "No parole."

"I'll wear an ankle monitor if it will make you happy."

"One more thing about mating, and I'll be quick because frankly, I'm about to explode, there is a… bite involved."

"How hard?"

He rubbed his red oak against me. "Pretty hard."

I smacked him. "The bite. How hard is the bite?"

"Do you want to find out?" The promise in his blue eyes made me nod. Vigorously.

"Yes." I wrapped my legs around his waist, inhaling sharply as his rigid log rolled against my throbbing pebble. "Do you love me, Ford?"

"I do."

"Good. I love you too."

"I think I saw that on one of my textbooks."

"Will you two get on with it already?" Tizzy asked, standing just outside the see-through shower door. "This is getting more *When Harry Met Sally* and less *When Hairy Wet*—"

"How in the world did you get in here?" Ford asked.

"Ask the witch," Tizzy said, pointing at me. "It was her translocation spell."

"Get out, Tiz!" I opened the door and threw a wet washcloth at her. When she raced, laughing, from the room, I turned to Ford. "That didn't kill the mood, did it?"

His love-lumber bumped against my girly-bits. "It'll take more than a sassy squirrel to put me off."

I rubbed against him, and he groaned, his spicy masculine aroma filling the shower stall. When the tip of him pressed against my opening, I rolled my hips, asking for more. I wanted him inside me like I wanted air to breathe.

"I don't think I can be gentle," he moaned.

"Then don't," I said. "I'm a tough girl."

His thumbs dug into my hips as he entered me inch by torturous inch. A helpless sound tumbled from my lips.

"I'm hurting you."

"No," I lied. His invasion inside me was painful—after all, he was a mountain of a man—but it would have hurt more for him to stop. "I want this, Ford. I want you."

"I do love you," he said. His teeth elongated. "More than I thought possible."

He bit down on my shoulder, and I screamed as a pleasure like nothing I've ever known ripped through my body as he pierced my flesh. He dropped to his knees, carrying me with him, and when my back was on the tile floor, he entered me completely and began to thrust in earnest.

Ecstasy wracked me with wave after wave of rapture as my orgasm spilled over me. Ford let go of my shoulder and roared as his own climax erupted, holding me until he'd spent every bit of himself inside me.

We lay there for Goddess knew how long before the water turned cold. Ford reached up and turned off the shower. "Mrs. Haze Baylor," he said teasingly, as he held me close.

"Is that a proposal?" My heart pounded like a fist against the inside of my chest.

"I'm yours for eternity, Haze. Until death do us part. Do you want to get married?"

"I do," I said.

"Then I do, too."

A loud knock on the bathroom door startled us. Next, a booming voice said, "You have your own shower in your own home, son."

"Dad?" Ford asked.

"Yes. Your mother wants me to congratulate you. So congratulations."

"Uhm, thanks." His cheeks were turning a very adorable shade of red.

"Welcome to the family, Hazel," Bryant Baylor said.

"Thank you, sir," I answered.

"Now get out," he demanded.

Ford stared down at me. "Why'd you pop us into my dad's shower?"

I shrugged. "How was I supposed to know it was your dad's shower? Didn't you notice?"

"I noticed your perky boobs. Everything else was a blur after that."

"I can hear you," Bryant added. "I'm getting

bleach. If you're not out by the time I get back, you will be getting cleaned along with the shower."

We stood up, wrapping ourselves in Mr. Baylor's towels. The one I had covered me from armpit to knees. On Ford, it looked more like a miniskirt.

Ford grimaced. "Can you get us out of here?"

"We're better off walking."

"You really are a terrible witch."

"But I'm an awesome lover, right?"

Ford grinned. "The best."

"I can still hear you," Bryant shouted.

I stared up at my mate. Three days had passed since I'd arrived back in my hometown, and a lifetime of events had occurred almost simultaneously. I had my best friend back, I no longer hated my father. Apparently, I was the new police chief, and the man of my dreams had promised to always love me. This was the first time that Paradise Falls didn't feel like a fail.

"I can see up your skirt, bear boy," Tizzy said. "Dang! You could put an eye out with that thing."

"Tizzy!"

She looked up at me, innocently batting her eyelashes. "You called?"

The End.

Start Reading Book 2: Rogue Coven today!

Rogue witches. Halloween pranks. Dead body. A hellmouth at the four-way between Main Street and Bliss.

Life in this paranormal town is anything but ordinary. As I settle into my new role as police chief and as the mate of the incredibly hunky werebear, Ford Baylor, I'm finding out just how chaotic things can get—especially around Halloween. It's the season of prank wars between the witches and the shifters, and I've got to put up with all the annoying shenanigans until one trick turns out to be deadly.

Now, I've got a murder to solve, protect Ford from rampant clown attacks, host a Halloween party for my squirrel familiar, and, oh yeah, shut down the hellmouth that's opened up in the middle of town. Just another day in Paradise Falls.

ROGUE COVEN - SNEAK PEEK
WITCHIN' IMPOSSIBLE COZY MYSTERIES
BOOK 2

Chapter One

"Puhleassssse, Hazel!" my squirrel familiar Tizzy said. Her tiny red-furred fingers were clasped together, and she was down on her little knees, blinking up at me with her large, lovely brown eyes. "It'll be All Hallows Eve in ten days. You know, the Devil's night, Hallowtide, *Nos Calan Gaeaf*."

I gave her a *WTF* look.

She threw her paws up in the air, her voice going higher pitched. "You're right, that Celtic reference was obscure even for me." She jumped from the kitchen counter, did a quick bounce on a diner stool, and landed with a skid across the marble center island. She stirred my coffee with one finger and cast her determined gaze up at me. "The point I'm trying to make is that Halloween is right around the corner!

It's only a week away. I really need a decision from you."

I flicked her paw away from my cup. "You're not turning our home into a haunted house."

Her chin dropped down to her chest, and her nose twitched. "You suck."

"I know, Tizzy. And I'm a terrible witch," I said, borrowing one of her favorite lines. Mostly because it was entirely true. I'd spent seventeen years avoiding my abilities while hiding in the human world as an FBI agent. Now that I was back in my hometown of Paradise Falls, and I could use my witchcraft freely, I found I still preferred my 9mm pistol to magic.

She stretched her arms wide with excitement as she went up on her tiny toes. "We could have smoke machines, cobwebs strung all over, bowls of eyeballs and guts, and spiders," she chirped. "Lots of big, fat, hairy spiders!" I must have gasped because she wiggled her fingers at me and said, "Unless that's a deal-breaker." She waved her hands in front of her chest. "Then no spiders."

"This is the first time in a very long time since we've had a real home, Tiz. We're not turning it into a sideshow attraction." Besides, the yearly prank wars between the witches and the shifters had already started, and I didn't want to paint a big old "Toilet Paper Me" sign on my house. I pointed at my persistent familiar. "I hate Halloween—a fact you've known since forever. Do you remember me ever having a decent time at Halloween in this town?"

"What about the prank wars between the shifter and witches? I want to win!" said Tizzy.

"Ugh. That's the Halloween tradition I hate the most."

Prank wars sucked. The pranks were fairly harmless in the sense that no one was allowed to use supernatural abilities to pull off a prank. It was mostly things like rubber snakes in public toilets, turning the high school football field's uprights upside down, and using soap to write all over cars. But sometimes they could get very elaborate. My senior year, a few shifters had entombed our crotchety school librarian's car, a VW Beetle, inside the cafeteria's walk-in refrigerator. Ms. Fredrickson still works at the high school. She's a witch, so she hasn't aged much at all, but she'd never had much in the way of magical power, so the shifters hadn't had their furry asses zapped by her. But there had been a lot of detention handed out.

I shook my head at the soulful expression on my familiar's face. "No."

Tizzy skittered up my arm and flicked my ear to get my attention. "This could be a great way for the town to get to know the new sheriff."

"Chief of police," I corrected, but only because

the Grand Inquisitor Clementine Battles, aka my grandmother, had insisted I take the job. I'd owed her two favors. Handling a thorn in her side, Adele Adams, had counted as favor number one, and staying in Paradise Falls and taking the job had been favor number two. She'd shown up in Paradise Falls twice since we'd fought a rogue witch who'd joined with some shifters to pull off some horrific druidic magic that included killing my best friend's brother and almost killing my friend as well. I was more grateful than I could say for her help, but I still harbored some major resentment for her part in jailing my dad. Her son. Ugh. Sure, everyone thought he'd murdered my mother, and no one could predict it was an unbinding spell gone wrong. However, Clementine was his mother. She should have protected him.

I shook my head. Maybe I'd lived out in the human world for too long. Maybe expecting a witch, especially an old one, to choose her child over her duty was too much to ask. If it came down to it, would my father choose me?

"I am the chief of police," I said again, mostly because it still sounded so weird to say it out loud.

The squirrel ignored me, obviously encouraged by this new line of thinking. "You know, it could be a total public relations event. All the little furbabies and witchlets and their parents—"

I shook my hands at her in a mock-scary wave. "Having the crap frightened out of them by a flying squirrel?" I took another sip of coffee, sweet with just the right amount of French vanilla creamer, but it had already started to cool down. "You realize the whole town is full of very real and very scary monsters, right? A bowl of noodles and peeled grapes isn't likely to impress anyone." We really had been gone from town too long if Tizzy thought anything about Halloween in Paradise Falls might resemble a human celebration.

"We could do a demon theme with splashes of blood all over the walls, some black light high-lighting ghostly handprints, and shrieking sound effects coming from the basement as if the bowels of hell have opened up to let all the demons out."

"That's not happening," a deep voice interrupted. "I like the color of my walls." Ford walked into the kitchen wearing tight jeans and a sky-blue tight t-shirt. Whew, damn, he made my libido zing.

"Our walls," I reminded my grumpy but undeni-ably sexy mate. "Good morning, Ford."

As I glanced at my mate, all six feet nine inches of him, I stifled a girlish giggle. I'd found out several months earlier that we were true mates, like shifter mates, even though I'm a witch. With shifters, it's a scent thing. To me, he smells like spicy desserts, and to him, I smell like vanilla and rum.

It's a long story that involves a sloppy, drunken kiss our senior year. How was I to know my bold, drunken move would imprint me on him? I was seventeen, for the love of red velvet cake. But looking at him now, I regretted nothing.

Except not spending the last seventeen years in his arms.

He was broad-shouldered, and his light blue eyes were bright in contrast to his chocolate-colored hair. It had grown out a couple of inches into a mop of thick curls. Just the way I liked it. There was nothing like grabbing a handful of his soft, silky mane while hollering his na— Uhm, you get my point. He had, however, shaved his short beard. Twice I'd gotten teased at the police station about the rug rash on my face, and that was enough to make me insist on him taking a razor to his scruff twice a day.

He kissed my cheek, and hot damn, the aroma of hot cinnamon rolls filled the air. I happily inhaled his scent as he poured himself a cup of coffee and sat down next to me at the center island. "Tizzy, we've been over this," he said.

Tiz balled her fingers into fists and put them on her hips. She gave me a pointed look. "Why does the bear get a say in this?"

"Because it's the bear's house," Ford said.

"Our house," I corrected, not admitting that his little slips of sole possession hurt my feelings.

"Our house," he amended.

I took a sip of my coffee. "Damn, it's cold already."

"Hello," Tizzy said. She pointed at me and wiggled her finger. "You should use your magic. It'll be good practice."

"Why would I do that when I can just pop the mug into the microwave. Easy-peasy."

Ford looked up from his newspaper. "Didn't you promise the council president you'd practice?"

The council president was my father, and yes, I had promised him I would work on my craft. I huffed a sigh. "Fine." I stared down at the offending cup of cold coffee and worked up a sufficient spell to cast before weaving the words that would make my witch's brew boil.

"Caffeine, caffeine, strong and bright.
You keep me going from morn 'til night.
I like you black, I like you sweet.
You're no good cold, so bring the heat.
Done is done, Goddess grant to me.
Steaming hot java, so mote it be."

Tizzy, Ford, and I leaned forward as the dark liquid began to boil.

"I think it's working, Haze," Tiz said excitedly.

I leaned back as rapidly churning bubbles began to form in the dark liquid. "Huh. I'm not sure that's right." Suddenly, the coffee began to hiss.

"Should it be fizzing?" Ford asked.

"That's not good," I stated as steam arose like a thick fog above the cup.

"Oh, my Goddess!" Tizzy shouted as Ford and I stood up, and the stools we'd been sitting on clattered to the stone tile floor.

"Get away from ground zero," I ordered Tiz.

She jumped from the center island to the sink counter in a blazing-quick leap while Ford and I stumbled back.

"It's going to blow!" Ford said.

We shielded our eyes against the impending disaster, all of us holding our breath while we waited for shattered pieces of the mug to go flying.

Nothing happened.

After a few seconds, I got brave enough to move back in for a second look. "Uh oh."

"What?" Ford asked. "What happened?"

I picked up the mug and tipped it sideways. The bottom was completely gone. Melted. There was a hole in the center island granite where the molten lava coffee had burned straight through. I opened the cabinet underneath. Tizzy scurried around my legs and peeked inside.

"Goddess, Haze. I hope that stuff doesn't burn a hole to China."

"It'll cool down before then." I hoped. "Or evaporate."

"It's magic," Tiz said. "It might not."

"Maybe we don't practice magic in the house anymore," Ford suggested.

I wanted to remind him that he was the one who poked me to do it in the first stupid place, but I settled for sticking my tongue out at him. "Good idea."

He strolled over to me, his hulking body dwarfing me as he gathered me in his arms. He cupped the back of my neck, stealing my breath, as he kissed me deeply and soundly.

I growled my pleasure, which earned me a decent bottom squeeze. Ford smiled at my dazed expression. "Now isn't that a much better use of your tongue?"

"Ha ha." I tried to keep my knees from buckling beneath me. I stroked my fingertips across the short hair on the back of his neck and leaned forward to press my boobs against his muscular chest. "Keep this up, Ford Baylor, and you're going to be late for work."

He grinned and winked at me. "That's okay. I sleep with the boss."

Tizzy jumped up on the center island again. "Ugh. I can't watch you two do the bear-witch boogie. It's too early in the morning. I'm going to Lily's."

Lily Mason, my childhood best friend and the

reason I was back in Paradise Falls, lived on the other side of town. Reluctantly, I slipped out of my mate's arms. "I'll drive you. I want to check in on Lily anyway." The reason I'd returned to Paradise Falls was to help Lily solve the mystery of her brother's death. She'd gotten the closure she deserved, but Danny had been the last of her family. I felt a keen responsibility to make sure she knew she wasn't alone.

I kissed Ford's cheek. "See you at the station."

He gestured to the center island. "Don't you think you should do something about the acid bath of coffee burrowing its way through the Earth's core?"

I looked at Tiz. "It should be...okay, right?"

She shrugged. "I'll support whatever lie you want to tell yourself."

"It's not a big deal." I bit my lower lip then let it go. "I'll ask my dad about it when I get a free minute. Until then, maybe we could use some of that super foam to plug the hole in the floor."

The lights in the kitchen flickered then went out.

"I think it just took out the electrical wiring, Haze," Ford said.

"Fine!" I threw up my hands. "I'll call Dad now."

Ford grabbed his truck keys. "And I'll take Tizzy to Lily's."

"Only if I get to pick the music," Tizzy said.

My bear man shook his head. "Nope."

"I will jump out the window if I have to listen to country or western," she whined.

Ford waved at her. "It was nice knowing you."

"Behave. Both of you," I called after them.

Tizzy followed Ford down the hallway to the front door, while giving a rapid dissertation on country music and the downfall of society.

Goddess, I loved that squirrel.

Download Book 2 Today

Read all the Witchin' Impossible Mysteries!
https://www.renee-george.com/
WitchinMysteries!

PARANORMAL MYSTERIES & ROMANCES
BY RENEE GEORGE

Witchin' Impossible Paranormal Mysteries

Witchin' Impossible (Book 1)

Rogue Coven (Book 2)

Familiar Protocol (Booke 3)

Mr & Mrs. Shift (Book 4)

FurOut (Book 5)

Barkside of the Moon Paranormal Mysteries

Pit Perfect Murder (Book 1)

Murder & The Money Pit (Book 2)

The Pit List Murders (Book 3)

Pit & Miss Murder (Book 4)

The Prune Pit Murder (Book 5)

Two Pits and A Little Murder (Book 6)

Pits and Pieces of Murder (Book 7)

Pittie Party Murder (Book 8)

Peculiar Mysteries & Romances

You've Got Tail (Book 1)

My Furry Valentine (Book 2)

Thank You For Not Shifting (Book 3)

My Hairy Halloween (Book 4)

In the Midnight Howl (Book 5)

Furred Lines (Book 6)

My Wolfy Wedding (Book 7)

Who Let The Wolves Out? (Book 8)

My Thanksgiving Faux Paw (Book 9)

Grimoires of a Middle-aged Witch

Earth Spells Are Easy (Book 1)

Spell On Fire (Book 2)

When the Spells Blows (Book 3)

Spell Over Troubled Water (Book 4)

Ghost in the Spell (Book 5)

Destiny of a Middle-aged Witch

Burning Djinn of Fire (Book 1)

Djinn Bottle Blues (Book 2)

Stand By Your Djinn (Book 3)

Nora Black Midlife Psychic Mysteries

Sense & Scent Ability (Book 1)

For Whom the Smell Tolls (Book 2)

War of the Noses (Book 3)

Aroma With A View (Book 4)

Spice and Prejudice (Book 5)

Age of Inno-Scents (Book 6)

Aroma Holiday (Book 7)

Vapes of Wrath (Book 8)

The Scented Cipher (Book 9)

Of Spice and Men (Book 10)

Hex Drive

Hex Me, Baby, One More Time (Book 1)

Oops, I Hexed It Again (Book 2)

I Want Your Hex (Book 3)

Hex Me With Your Best Shot (Book 4)

Hex Me All Night Long (Book 5)

ABOUT THE AUTHOR

USA Today Bestselling Author, Renee George writes paranormal mysteries and romances because she loves all things whodunit, Other-worldly, and weird. Also, she wishes her pittie, the adorable Kona, could talk. Or at least be more like Scooby-Doo and help her unmask villains at the haunted house up the street.

When she's not writing about mystery-solving

werecougars or the adventures of a hapless psychic living among shapeshifters, she dons her superhero cape and rescues kittens. Okay, the kitten totally showed up one day and suddenly she's got a new pet named Simon.

She lives in Missouri with her family and spends her non-writing time doing really cool stuff...like watching TV and cleaning up dog poop.

Join My Newsletter

Follow Me On Bookbub!

Join Renee's Rebel Readers on Facebook!